The Black Bishop

Copyright © 2001 John Moody
All rights reserved.

ISBN 1-58898-533-4

The Black Bishop

John Moody

greatunpublished.com
Title No. 533
2001

The Black Bishop

ACKNOWLEDGEMENTS

Some years ago, a dear friend of mine, Abe Thomy (who is a man of a thousand talents) and I were discussing his book TIN GOD. Abe shared with me an idea for a book that I found tempting and, since he offered me the idea for the taking, I accepted. Thanks Abe.

There were others I wish to thank. My wife, Maggie, Drs. Don and April Gordon, friends extraordinaire and both outstanding PhDs in their fields, Shirley Humphries and many others, not for their input, of course, but for their encouragement and their kind criticisms.

For most authors writing a book is its own reward. When one is published, the rewards are manifold. I could name many others like Bill and Rebecca, Laura, Lee Ray, Lide, and the entire rest of my extended family.

THANKS TO YOU ALL. I LOVE YOU VERY MUCH.

FORWARD

This is a work of fiction. Though not impossible to have happened, it did not. The characters, the names, and many of the places are figments of my imagination. I have taken some liberties with the times and events. Essentially, however, the framework of history has not been altered.

I started out to write a humane story about good people. Naturally, though unfortunately, the inclusion of evil men and events was necessary. Somehow, even in the worst of times, goodness does prevail. Often it prevails only in principle. It is truly unfortunate that evil moves about freely when goodness is absent, but goodness must always do battle with evil. You may note the somewhat rapid movement of the story line. This is for two reasons. First, is my many years of writing short stories and, secondly, because I abhor long dull pages written simply to increase volume.

ENJOY!

*To Maggie
My beloved wife
The most beautiful girl in the world.*

*To Brenden
My grandson
Barely two years old and already a better man than I.*

*And to Steppney Gregg
My oldest and dear friend
One of the first free-born blacks.
Sleep well old friend.*

CHAPTER 1

Jason Appelligo sat high in the church loft with a group of the other slaves of the Manigault Plantation. He was only nine, so he did not fully realize why he and his people sat packed into the stifling heat of the upper sanctuary while the white planters sat in the cool, sparsely populated, main floor. It was no matter, though. Jason loved coming. The things the Minister said were fascinating to him. He tried to listen intently to every word. He couldn't hear enough about all of God's wonderful promises and about the people who had seen and known him.

There was one distraction, however. When the Minister's voice rose in shrillness to a certain pitch, which it often did, the rafters rang in resonance, almost to the point of being painful. Jason wondered if the fancy dressed people in the richly carved pews could hear it too.

Jason looked down and caught the eye of Fitzsimmons Manigault, Jr., his friend. They winked at each other, and then Jason placed his attention back on the Minister's sermon.

Fitz was in stark contrast to Jason. They were the same age. As a matter of fact, they were both born on the same night... Fitz in the big house on fine, crisp sheets with a doctor attending...and Jason under the stars on an old blanket with Mattie, the black mid-wife, yelling instructions.

Fitzsimmons, Sr., master of the Manigault plantation, often stated that it was the worst night of his life. People were aware that Fitz's birth had been hard on his mother but no permanent damage was done. On the other hand, Jason knew nothing about his birth. No one ever mentioned it.

Except for sharing the same birthday there was no similarity between the two boys. Fitz was dressed in highly polished leather boots, dark brown riding pants, and a beautifully tailored jacket that left a hint of his ruffled shirt and silk tie. Jason's rough, hand woven coat hung in baggy hugeness over his homespun shirt. His shoes, once Fitz's, pinched his toes and made walking an exercise in pain. He was glad he only had to wear them to church.

The Minister began a long prayer and Jason's mind began to wander.

From the earliest moment Jason could remember, he and Fitz had been constant companions. His mother had been Fitz's wet nurse. The two of them had always been together, even suckling in unison. As toddlers they would sit together on the dock in front of the house and fish patiently for hours for the bream and catfish that abounded in the river. When they were older and could think of all kinds of mischief, it was Fitz who led them into constant difficulty and Jason who followed and shared in the discipline. They knew each other's every secret. Many times they knew each other's every thought. When Fitz started school Jason would wait impatiently for the tutor to leave, and even more impatiently for Fitz to finish his assignments and emerge from the house. Then, together, they would be off to new adventures along the river's edge or in the dark, heavy swamps that surrounded the huge plantation.

Once they saw a bobcat and chased him with the sticks their imaginations saw as gleaming swords with which they pledged themselves to keep the world safe. They watched the squirrels at play. They studied the crows. On occasion, they world see an alligator swimming lazily in the river. The grown-ups laughed and said they were floating logs. But to Fitz and Jason they were dragons.

Finally the minister screamed "Amen". The blacks quietly filed out of the balcony, through the back door, and into the forest for the long walk back to the plantation.

Jason liked the walk home. As soon as they reached the cover of the trees he could remove his shoes. He usually played hide and seek along the way with the other children. The older folk would break into song. They would sing their own songs with the words they understood so well, and the masters did not understand at all.

These were good times. The forest smelled sweet with the heavy odor or honeysuckle but not so heavy that the air could not lift the soft, harmonic voices of the blacks.

"Poor Fitz", Jason would think. "He has to stand around the church and listen to the ladies' silly giggles and the men talk like pompous asses". At least, that's what Fitz had said.

"What's pompous?" Jason asked.

"They think they're so much!" Fitz had responded.

"So much what?"

"So rich and so smart."

"Oh."

"And the minister always has to eat with us and I can't change my clothes for hours and hours. Jason, you got it good."

"Yeah."

CHAPTER 2

Fitzsimmons Manigault senior had a hard and fast rule. No slave child was put to work prior to the age of fifteen. It was but one of the may rules he made to operate his plantation on a humane basis. But it had puzzled Jason.

"How come we don't have to work 'til we fifteen?" Jason asked Fitz. "All the other plantations works they chillen."

"Why don't, not why come," said Fitz, who was seriously concentrating on whittling a stick at the time. "And it's their children."

"Why don't we have to work 'til we fifteen?" Jason corrected himself and admired the new jack knife.

"I don't know," Fitz said, and blew a shaving from the stick.

"Ax yo' Daddy."

"Ask your Daddy, Jason. It's ask, not ax. And it's your, not yo."

"Ask your Daddy."

"There's no need. He doesn't know either. He just says children should have a childhood."

One day, they sat fishing on the riverbank. "How come, I mean, Why do you have to go to school and I don't, Fitz?"

"Because a white man has to know how to read."

"Do a Negro need to know how to read?"

"Does, Jason, does."

"Does a Negro need to know how to read?"

"I don't know. Probably not."

Fitz stared across the river for a long moment, deep in thought. Finally he looked at his friend, his eyes dancing.

"Hey Jason! You want to learn to read? I can teach you. It would be fun. I could be the teacher and you could be me and I could teach you everything I know. It would be fun!"

Jason became excited. Then his face fell.

"Seems like mama said we ain't suppose to know how to read."

Fitz grew serious.

"Seems like that's right. But it's probably because you don't need to know."

"Maybe we better not, Fitz. It might get us in trouble."

Fitz's eyes flashed a sly glint and a smile crossed his face. He liked the challenge and he liked the danger he could only sense.

"It doesn't matter. I'll teach you any way. No body has to know but us. We'll make a blood pact. Where's my jack knife?"

"Do we have to do that again? We already blood brothers. We already blood pacted on 'bout everything."

"OK. This time we'll just spit and swear."

So they spat and they swore. And, for good measure, they spat again.

The very following afternoon, Fitz bought a book with him to their secret hide out.

"This is an old Bible, Jason. It's the only book I can find to sneak out of the house. There are so may of them mama won't miss it. Daddy bought a hundred for the church last year. I bet we have twenty just like it left over."

They did not know just how terribly forbidden teaching Jason to read was, but they sensed it, they had all along. So they kept it secret with a vengeance. They worked in private, away from everyone. Sometimes they worked behind the barn, but mostly they worked in their secret place near the river's edge where they could watch all the approaches from their well concealed hiding place.

"The first thing you need to know is your ABC's."

Jason was puzzled. "What's an Abeesy."

"A B C 's, not Abeesy."

"What they is?"

"You mean what are they."

It was hard for Fitz to explain, but Jason learned them anyway. How to say them, how to recognize them, how to reproduce them on the sandy floor of their hide out.

"I don't think you need to know how to write, just read," Fitz said. "But I can't figure out how to teach you one without the other. I guess they just kind of go together."

Fitz was a brilliant child but, in truth, his intellect paled in comparison to Jason's awakening mind. At the end of only a few weeks, by the time they had completed the laborious process of sounding out Genesis, the words began to form thoughts, pictures, and ideas in Jason's mind. Already it was not a matter of letters and words for him. It was concepts. It was knowledge!

One warm summer afternoon, when they were ten, they were lazily drifting down the river. The old burlap sail on their homemade raft hung limply in the stillness. Fitz, squinting in the southern sun, slapped at the mosquitoes. Jason's whole consciousness, as well as his nose, was buried in his Bible.

Finally, in frustration, Fitz said, "Judas Priest, Jason! Would you put that book down and let's play something? The mosquitoes are eating me alive. Jason...JASON!"

Jason looked up, oblivious to what Fitz had said.

"People don't talk like 'dat."

"That", Fitz corrected. "What are you talking about."

"Thee and Thou and that way."

"I know. But they did in the olden days." Fitz thought for a moment, adding to his squint. "And maybe God talks like that. Just remember thee is you and thy is your and stuff like that.

"What is Selah?"

"Forget that one, it doesn't mean anything."

"How do you know?"

"'Cause Papa said so."

The raft had drifted into some back water. It dragged lightly against the bottom.

"We better start poling back", Fitz said. "It will soon be supper time. We're having leg of lamb for supper. What are you havin' Jason?"

"Greens, I guess", Jason said, returning to his book.

"Put that book down, Jason. I'm not gonna do all the polin" by myself."

Reluctantly Jason wrapped and tied his Bible in the sheet of oiled leather Fitz had given him in case they capsized. He picked up his pole, but his mind was still dwelling 2,000 years in the past.

It had started as a game for Fitz, playing school teacher to his friend. But for Jason, it was no game. He never tired of it. New experiences opened to him. New adventures, new ideas, and new friends created a strange and exciting world in his mind. David became his ideal as the dashing, powerful hero. Moses became his father figure. He would walk through the forest on the way home from church and watch for the bushes to burst into flame, at least one bush, and speak to him. He would stand by the river's edge and concentrate until his head hurt trying to part the water. More than once he tried to walk on the water only to sink into the slimy bottom.

"I guess I ain't got enough of the faith yet", he would think to himself. Then he would pray for God to help him with his lack of faith and give him a sign.

He lived and breathed his school book, this precious Bible that Fitz had inscribed: "To Jason, From your friend forever, Fitz."

To Fitz it had been fun, to Jason it was fun too, but it became more as time went on. It was a direction. It was freedom. It gave him power that he could not comprehend, only feel.

"Let's go fishing tomorrow, Jason." Fitz finally awakened him from his thoughts.

"What about my lesson?"

"We can do both at the same time. I'll teach you history and geography tomorrow when we go squirrel hunting."

"Awright."

"Don't slur your "l's", Jason. Alright"

"All right, all right all right. Where do you hear all this stuff about how to talk anyway?"

"It's what Mama and Papa tell me, Jason, and the tutor, too."

"Hey you. Boy!"

Fitz and Jason froze. On the near bank stood two men. They were unshaven and shabbily dressed. They held rifles and there were knives in their belts. With them was a third man, a Negro. He was in chains. His head was bowed but the boys could see one eye swollen shut and heavy crusts of blood on his face and shirt.

"That yo' nigger, Boy? Or is yo' heppin' a runaway?"

Fitz and Jason had been repeatedly warned about these kinds of men. They were suddenly very frightened. Fitz bravely said: "He's my nigger and this is my father's land, the Manigault Plantation, and you had better get off of it."

"The Manigault, huh? Which way is the Island Belle?"

"About four miles down river," Fitz answered.

"You sho' that's yo' nigger?" the man asked again. He tossed his rifle to the other man, stepped into the edge of the backwater, and began walking toward them. The boys' nervous reaction made him suspicious.

Fitz, and certainly Jason, knew about runaway hunters. They were violent men. "The backwash trash of the south" according to Fitzsimmons senior.

Suddenly Fitz's fright overcame him.

"Pole, Jason, pole!"

The boys desperately began leaning on the poles to move their awkward raft. The man dashed through the water. Grabbing the raft, he picked up the edge and dumped both boys into the river's shallows. Fitz came up spitting muddy water and swinging wildly at his adversary. The man backhanded Fitz knocking him sprawling, and reached for Jason who was oblivious to everything but rescuing the Bible. Jason clutched the leather bound package just as the man scooped him up from the water.

"We got us another one," he laughed. When he turned to show his partner their newly captured "runaway", the smile drained from his face. The water trickled from his hair and down across his eyes as they grew cold as steel.

"I recken that's enough."

It was the Manigault overseer, Jonathan Mitchell. His Tennessee walker pawed the moist earth quietly as Jonathan met the cold stare of the intruder. The first thing the intruder noticed was the blue steel of his pistol as Jonathan scratched his temple with the barrel. Then he saw his partner standing helplessly, a rifle in each hand, with a half dozen Manigault slaves standing around him. The sharp edges of their tools glistened in the sunlight.

"I jest caught me a runaway nigger, thass all," the man spouted.

"You just assaulted the master's son and his "boy," Jonathan said softly. But his face was not soft.

The man looked from the overseer to his partner, who still stood frozen. In order for his partner to fire, he would have to drop one rifle, raise the other, cock and fire. He would be cut down by the overseer's pistol or hacked to death by the Manigault slaves long before he could do that. Slavers were, for the most part, docile on the Manigault Plantation because they were treated with more care and dignity than in most places. But they were not docile when faced with defending Jason and Fitz or backing Jonathan.

The man broke into a broad grin and gently released Jason.

"Honest mistake," he said. "You can't blame a man for an honest mistake."

"Mastah Mitchull, this here's Jethro!" the chained Negro whispered.

"Jethro? You sure? That you, Jethro?"

"Yessa. This here's Jethro."

Jonathan glared at the intruder. "What are you doing with the Island Belle's head house nigger?"

"We caught him near Charleston runnin' away with two damn fine horses and a bran' new carriage."

"That right, Jethro?" Jonathan dismounted and went over to

him. He holstered his weapon, but two of his bucks had taken position by the armed intruder, thus the intruder's dilemma continued. He remained frozen.

"I wus fetchin' Miss Lilly, only I didn't git there yet."

"My God, Jethro, you're beat all to hell."

"I think my ribs is busted, Massa Mitchull."

Jonathan turned, his eyes spitting fire. "You son's of bitches", he yelled. "Billy, you and Mo-duck take Jethro to the clinic. Here, put him on my horse. Fitz, you and Jason git on home."

Jason and Fitz scrambled back onto the raft and began poling out of the backwater toward the house. Jonathan, Billy and Mo-duck gently raised Jethro into the saddle.

At that instant, with their backs to him, the intruder dropped one of the rifles, raised and cocked the other with one motion for a shot at Jonathan's back. But there was no shot. The only sound heard was the quiet "swoosh" and a cracking sound like an ax through a coconut. The stare of surprise was still on his face when Big Mumbo went over and retrieved the hatchet from his skull.

"You bastards will pay for this! That there's my nigger! And that big nigger just murdered my brother. Goddamn it!"

Big Mumbo took a step toward him, the muscles rippling in the forearm holding the blooded hatchet. The man, back peddling, fell sprawling in the shallow water.

"No, Mumbo, Wait!" Jonathan said. He walked into the water and lifted the man by his lapels.

"Listen, you foul breath son of a bitch. That over there is the best-loved nigger in these parts. He wasn't running away. You and your buddy beat the hell out of him for the fun of it. Then you trespass on Manigault land and attack the master's son. Then your partner tries to kill me. Now you give me one good reason why I shouldn't hang you from that big oak." He nodded to a magnificent angel oak fifty yards away. "On second thought, you shouldn't hang, especially from that beautiful tree. I'll just leave you with Big Mumbo and go on home. You can beat him up, maybe break his ribs."

The man's fear stripped him of words. He stared, opened

mouthed, at Big Mumbo. No one had ever bothered to measure or weigh Big Mumbo, but there was no doubt of his size. He was a mountain of muscle and sinew that rippled and heaved under his blue-black skin. He said very little. Normally his eyes spoke for him. And, at that moment, having just killed a man, they shone so that even Jonathan was uncomfortable watching them.

"No sir, it were a mistake. My brother there, he done it. He done it all. I told him not to. I begged him..."

"What's your name?"

"Bobby T."

"Bobby T. what?"

"Bobby T. Jordan."

"Well, Bobby T. Jordan, I'm gonna turn you loose. Now if I ever see, or even hear tell of you again, I'm sending Big Mumbo looking for you. I'm gonna tell him to bring me back your head for bar-b-queing. Now git!" For emphasis, he plowed his fist into Bobby T.'s face. Again, he went sprawling into the water.

Scrambling to his feet and running hard, he soon disappeared into the woods.

"Ya'll bury this one over there by the oak", Jonathan said. "Mark it in case the sheriff wants to see. I'm going to check on Jethro and get word to the Island Belle."

By this time Jason and Fitz had poled their way back to the pier at the main house. They were both still shaking from their brush with the runaway hunters. They were so shaken, that they said nothing to anyone. They went tearing straight for their hide out.

The first thing Jason did when he reached the hide out was tooo unwrap his Bible and make sure it was OK. To his great relief it was fine. Fitz dug through their "stuff" until he found his jack knife.

"I wish I had had this with me," Fitz said, brandishing the knife. "I'd have split his gullet."

Jason just grunted and continued trying to get his breath.

That evening both boys were sternly lectured at length about their wandering ways and were ordered to stay close to where they could be watched and protected. Of course, the trauma of the day soon wore off and their lives returned to normal. No mention was ever made of the incident again. The sheriff never even bothered to come out to the plantation.

CHAPTER 3

The months passed slowly and lazily for the boys. Though they played hard, they worked hard also on Jason's "schooling".

"What is it you and Massa Fitz does all day, boy?" Jason's mother asked one evening. Meta was her name. She was tall and slim and intelligent. She ran the big house with flawless precision. Jason's father, Abraham, was the butler. Officially, he was in charge, but Meta actually ran things.

"Jest play, mama." Jason felt the proper English he was learning fall away into the more acceptable way of speaking. This did not surprise him. His mother did the same thing between her duties at the house and the slave quarters.

"Jest play? Lord ya'll play a lot."

"I looks affa him like I spose to. I'se really workin' sted of playin'."

"Well, I worry ya'll spend too much time together. Ya'll might become too gooder friends."

"We is friends, mama. Fitz is my best friend in the whole world. We'd do anything for each other."

"I'm mighty sorry to hear that, Jason. Fitz is a good boy. But he the Massa's son. By the time ya'll growed up, you'll be jest another nigger workin' this place. I hate to think of the hurt you'll have to go through.

"Don't worry, Mama. Fitz ain't like that."

She looked at him with sad eyes and shook her head.

By the time Jason and Fitz were almost fifteen, they had been studying in secret, daily, for several years. Jason knew his Bible far better than anyone in the church, to include the minister. He still listened to the words in church even though he had no need. He knew whole books of the Bible by heart, especially the Gospels. His vast intellect absorbed worlds of information from the short, concise passages. Jason did not yet understand that by learning to read in his Bible he was among the most informed biblical scholars in the entire south. His tremendous intellect, coupled with his simple acceptance of the truth, gave him understanding few could ever hope to have. Nor did he understand how completely the rest of his life was being shaped by his reading lessons.

One Sunday Jason looked down at Fitz. Fitz's eyes caught his, but this time they did not smile. Something was wrong. Jason could see a great sadness permeating his friend's face.

After church, and a sumptuous meal with the minister and other invited guests, Fitz went to the hideout. Jason was waiting. He watched Fitz approaching with head down, stooped shoulders and a dragging step that was alien to his young energetic friend.

Fitz sat down with a heavy sigh.

"What's wrong, Fitz?"

"Nothing."

"Something."

Fitz looked at Jason and the tears welled up in his eyes.

"Papa says I have to go away."

"Away? Where? Charleston?"

"I wish. No. To Europe."

"Europe? Ain't that across the ocean?"

"Isn't. You mean isn't. Actually to England."

"Why?"

"To School."

"There are plenty of schools in Charleston. Good ones too. You said so. Did you tell him that?"

Silence.

"Well, tell him Fitz!"

"Mama and Papa called me into the library last night and we had a long talk. Papa said 'you're almost fifteen years old now. It's time you went away to school.' I tried to talk him out of it. I told him Mr. Andrews was a good teacher, but he said 'no'. I told him I didn't want to go to Charleston.

Fitz sighed again. "Papa said 'No, Fitz. I'm afraid it won't be Charleston. You will go to England.' I started crying and then Papa did too." He said, 'Fitz, war is coming and I've a big job for you. I've taken every penny I can spare and invested it in Europe. There is no question about it. When war comes, the south will be stripped bare. That's why I've done it. Our money is already safely invested in Europe. You must be there as a representative for our family's investment for the future'."

I said, "But who will we fight Papa? What do you mean? I don't understand. What happens in a war?"

He said, "Fitz, the abolitionists will soon have their way. A man named Lincoln will probably be the next President, and he will want to free the slaves. When he does, our economy will be destroyed. Life as we know it will fade into history as a very "ignoble experiment".

"What does that mean?" Jason asked, desperately trying to understand, to make some sense out of what was happening.

"Papa said it means slavery never was a good idea, not even from an economical standpoint."

"I don't understand that either."

"It isn't right to have slaves, Jason. But now that we do, we can't change it."

"Why not?"

"Because there isn't enough money to profit them and keep the plantation running."

"Oh," Jason said. But he really didn't understand.

"Papa explained it all to me last night. The Yankees will come and they'll free you and you wont have anywhere to go or know how to make a living. You'll starve to death."

"I'll go to Charleston and get me a job and make me lots of money and have my own horse and buggy, and…"

"What job, Jason? What can you do?"

"Lots of stuff."

"And what about everybody else? They don't pick cotton in Charleston. They don't plant rice or even have vegetable gardens. Papa says he wants slaves to be free, too, but it will take years and millions and millions of dollars to prepare them and the society for it."

"What's the society?"

"White folks."

"Oh."

"Anyway, Papa talked a long time. Mama too. I'll be leaving in the fall."

"What am I gonna do?"

"We'll be fifteen. You'll be working."

"In the fields?"

"No!" Fitz's eyes grew hard. "I won't let them do that to you! Papa promised to make you a stable boy and footman. That way you'll eat at the big house and become a house nigger later."

"Thank you, Fitz."

"You're welcome. What is 369 divided by 39?"

Jason thought for a moment. "Nine with eighteen left over."

"In decimals."

Jason thought again. "Nine point four six."

"Good. When was the Battle of Hastings?"

"1066."

"Good. Of course, everyone knows that one."

The lessons had begun. All talk of their coming separation was forgotten for the moment.

The rest of the summer was much as summers past. The boys played and studied together. They had many adventures, great and small, all confined to their fantasy world. Bobby T. was barely a memory now. As far as anyone knew, he had left that part of the country.

"It's cold out here today, Jason."

"I don't care, Fitz. I love this place. It's so beautiful looking at the river. Someday I'm gonna build me a cabin right here on this spot and sit on the porch and watch the river forever."

"That's not likely, Jason."

"Why not?"

"We're practically in the shadow of Manigault House. Papa wouldn't let you build a cabin here.

CHAPTER 4

The day after Jason's fifteenth birthday, he reported to the stables. Jonathan was there waiting for him.

"Jason, this is where you'll work. Now Samson here is the head man. You do as he says. Right, Samson?"

"Yas, suh, Massa Mishull."

"Jason ought to make you a good man, Samson. OK, lets go to work."

"Come on, boy." Samson led Jason to the stall where Bonny, Jonathan's Tennessee Walker, was waiting.

"Yo' always saddles Bonny fust. If Massa Mishull want a diffrunt one, he'll tell yo."

"Yas suh, Samson."

"Don't 'suh' me boy. Is you know how to saddle a hoss?"

"No suh, I mean, no."

"Den you watch me dis time."

Jason watched. Finally he asked the obvious. "How am I gonna reach way up there?"

"Use de stool."

"Is it hard to tighten that thing?"

"De cinch. Don't worry, Massa Mishcull will tighten he own cinch. You jest put it through so as it don' fall off. Now you leads him out front o' de barn and hitch him to de post."

Jason spent the rest of the day shoveling, raking, putting down fresh hay, feeding, currying, brushing, combing, watering, washing, straightening, and a hundred other things.

"There's a lot of work in a stable", he said to Samson.

Samson smiled, nodded his head in agreement and continued repairing the harness on his work table.

"When will I have to do all this again? Nex' week?"

"Tomorrow."

"Tomorrow?"

Samson smiled again. "Tomorrow, and every day after that, ceptin' Sunday."

Jason ached all over. The thought of working that hard every day was a little more than frightening.

"It's almost supper time. Can I go home now?"

"You can quit after you takes care of Bonny. Massa Mishull always de las' one back. After you takes care of Bonny, you go to de kitchen. Dey will feed you. Then you can go home."

It was almost dark when Jonathan handed Bonny's reins to Jason. It was another hour before he finished his work.

When Jason was in the kitchen, stirring the food in his plate, too tired to eat, Fitz came in and sat down beside him.

"Whew! Jason, you smell awful!"

"Yeah."

"Well, how did it go?"

"It was alright."

"I bet you're glad I got you easy work in the stable."

Jason looked at him. Then he burst out laughing. He had suddenly realized something about being white and being black. He wasn't sure what, but it was something so horrible that it had made him laugh.

Three days later Jason moved into a little room in the loft of the stable.

"Dease is important animals", Samson said. "I sleep down here close to them. I want you here too."

It was like leaving home for Jason. He saw his parents now and then when he was in the kitchen eating. They would wave or smile, but they seldom had time to stop and speak to him. He was home sick. He would lie on his cot at night and cry himself to sleep. If he had had some light, he could have read his Bible. But there was no light. Certainly, he could not ask for one to read by. A lantern in the stables was forbidden.

The second Saturday he was working, Samson called him to his little room.

"Tomorrow's Sunday. You gonna be footman tomorrow."

Jason shook his head yes. He had watched the footmen before.

"Now, try this on."

It was his uniform. Very fancy. It was clean and pressed. The boots were high and shiny black. Most surprisingly, every thing almost fit.

"Where's Hambone? How come he ain't footin' tomorrow?"

"Hambone's sick. Besides, Massa say you spose to foot so you might as well start. Now, is you know what to do?"

"Not exactly."

"I'se de driver. I"se in charge. Now when you sees the Massa comin', or the lady, or who ever's ridin', you open de door and stands dere straight as a stick. When they sits, you close de do' and come 'round and jump up here. When we gits dere, you jumps off and opens de do'. You understand?"

"I understand."

"Two things to remember. When they gitten in or out, you bows, like dis." Samson demonstrated a slight bow with his eyes cast down.

"What's the other thing?"

"Keep yo' mouth shet. I don't want to hear a sound out of you, not even if you fall off. Now let me see you do it. I'll ack like the Massa."

They ran through it several times until Samson was satisfied. The following morning Jason stood proudly beside the carriage door when the family descended the steps of the big house. He was letter perfect. Even when Fitz tried to talk to him he remained silent and stared straight ahead.

As Jason became more accustomed to his duties he became more efficient. Within a month he was finding an hour a day to read his Bible. Fitz would come to his loft and they would talk and, sometimes, study.

"I won't need these when I leave, Jason, so I brought them to you", Fitz said one day.

It was a slate and several pens, ink, paper and a math book. Jason hid them in an old crate in the corner of his room. Now he could practice writing more. But he would practice on the slate. The pens, ink, and paper were precious items that could not be used foolishly.

"You can write me in England. I'll send you my address," Fitz had said.

CHAPTER 5

The day Fitz left for England was cloudy and dark with a misty, soaking rain. It was very normal weather for late summer on the Manigault plantation.

Jason stood by the carriage door waiting for Fitz, his livery already soaked from the constant, blowing rain. His face, covered with water droplets, hid the tears that slipped from his eyes and down his cheeks.

Fitz and his father soon emerged from the house. Fitz's mother and all the household staff came onto the porch and stood among the columns to bid their farewells. When they reached the carriage, Fitz turned to his father and said: "Papa, I want Jason to ride inside with us."

Fitzsimmons hesitated.

"Please, Papa. It's raining, and I won't see him for a long time."

"Get in, Jason." Fitzsimmons closed the door himself, getting in last.

On the porch Meta's eyebrows went up and Abraham stared coldly.

The high stepping team pulled the carriage away smartly. The baggage wagon that followed lumbered awkwardly.

Jason was terribly uncomfortable sitting inside with the two Manigaults, but Fitz's constant chatter, and the occasional grabbing of his hand, soon helped him relax. Fitz senior showed no indication of disapproval. That helped, too.

"Jason, there are so many things we need to talk about. I'm going to be gone a long, long time. Now, you have to take care of the raft, and it needs a new sail. I want you to keep my squirrel gun clean for me. Is that alright, Papa?"

He didn't wait for an answer but continued on with his admonitions to Jason to maintain things so that nothing would change in his absence. He wanted everything to stand still while he was gone, nothing to change, so that he could resume life on the Manigault someday as though not a moment had passed. Fitz knew that was futile. But he was fighting his grief. Part of the process was to deny that time passes, people and things change. He would never recapture the lazy, care-free life he was leaving, but he could not face that now. Jason responded to the illusion. He, too, did not want change. Fitzsimmons senior listened, though he appeared not to. He understood what was going on.

Fitz never stopped talking the entire four-hour trip to Charleston. He rattled on and on with the "don't forgets", the "be sure to's", and the "when I get backs".

When the carriage stopped on the wharf, Fitz became silent. His features fell. His forced smile and his animated gestures evaporated.

"You boys wait here in the carriage", Fitzsimmons said. "I'll see to the baggage loading and your accommodations, Fitz."

When the door closed Fitz looked at Jason with tears in his eyes. In a hushed voice he said: "Jason, you've got to look after Mama and Papa for me. If they free you while I'm gone, you've got to promise me you won't leave them. At least, not 'til I get back."

"I won't Fitz. I'll look after 'em real good, too." His voice broke.

Dabbing his sleeve at his tears, Fitz fumbled in his pocked with the other hand.

"Here, Jason." He held the jack knife out for Jason to take. It wasn't new and shiny anymore, it was somewhat the worst for wear. But it was the prized jack knife. "You'll need this for all kinds of stuff, especially when you work on the raft."

Jason took it and examined it with the wonder and admiration appropriate for a fifteen year old.

"I'll take real good care of it, Fitz. I won't lose it or break it or nothin'. When you get it back, it will be gooder than new."

"Better, not gooder. No, Jason. It's a present. It's yours forever and ever. I don't want it back."

"Gosh! Thanks, Fitz." Suddenly the knife was shiny new in his eyes. He had never owned such a wonderful thing, except his Bible, of course. But that was different. Jason now had a second possession.

"Fitz, you're my best friend in the whole world."

"And you're my best friend, Jason. We will always be best friends. We got a blood pact. Remember?"

Jason looked down at the knife again. "Yeah, I remember. It's this scar right here." He showed him the top-most one on his wrist.

Fitzsimmons senior opened the carriage door. "Come on, Fitz." Then he called up to the driver: "Samson, you all go home. I'm staying in town for a meeting. I'll be coming home tomorrow with Mr. Daxalt.

"Yassa, Massa Fitz."

Jason watched as the two Fitzs went up the gangplank of the magnificent sailing ship.

"Git yo' black ass up here with me, boy", Samson called down. "It ain't fittin."

CHAPTER 6

That evening, at the Gilmore House, Fitz was escorted to the library by the black butler. There were a dozen men in the room, some of the most important men in all of South Carolina's low country. The meeting had already begun.

"The north has been strangling us to death with their tariffs for years and years. With all these damn free states, they can out vote us on every issue, and they are!" said the Honorable Judge Lambeau.

Matthew Johnson rose from his seat. "For God's sake, Judge. The tariff issue has always been worth seceding over, but we never have. States rights is a thing of the past. There are no states rights, and there is no state that can secede alone. They'd be occupied within a week by Federal troops."

Matthew had fought the north's dictation of the nation's direction for years. He never experienced a victory in his fight and his frustration and bitterness showed.

"Well, Fitz, what do you think? Will we secede?" the Judge asked.

Fitz seated himself and accepted a brandy from the butler.

"I'm afraid so, your honor. We're not talking about just money this time. We're talking about our survival as a society."

"Afraid so, Fitz? Afraid?" asked James Lionell.

"I suppose afraid is a good choice of words," Fitz responded. "It was unconscious on my part. But yes, I am afraid so."

"Nonsense!" cried Horace McGill. "Let them invade! We'll kick their tails back across the Potomac in six weeks."

"Here, Here!" several voices chimed in.

"With what? Asked the Judge. "We have no iron works, no powder factories. We don't even have a stockpile of military equipment. All we have is our squirrel guns and dress swords."

"We'll take them from the Yankees." McGill retorted. "There's the powder magazine, there's Fort Sumter, there's Fort Moultrie and there's Castle Pinckney."

"Even if those supplies would last a week, Horace, how do we take them? They are forts, you know," said the Judge.

"Only Moultrie is garrisoned."

"True, but if things grow more tedious, they'll take all available supplies and move to Sumter. Mark my words."

As the conversation continued, it became obvious to Fitz that nothing would be accomplished here. Of course, he knew nothing could be. This was only intellectualism riddled with unreality. Meetings like this were going on all over the South. They would accomplish very little other than let some of the people vent their feelings.

"...And every decent officer in the army is a southerner," McGill continued. "We're better horsemen, better shots, and far better qualified to command."

"A manufacturing society will demolish an agrarian one in a war and you know it." The Judge was getting angry.

"Not if we engage and prevail quickly. We can, and we will."

Louis Gilmore, the host, stood. "Gentlemen. I find your arguments fascinating and, ah, enlightening, but we must get on with the purpose of the meeting. And that is money. It always seems to come down to money. Have you noticed?" he laughed.

"Well we can't create and finance our own government without it, and that's the truth," said Horace McGill.

"How true, Horace," Gilmore continued. "Now, if I might have our pledges, gentlemen, I'll see that they are properly routed." Each man handed Gilmore an envelope.

"Thank you, gentlemen. I've had a light meal prepared for us. Perhaps we'll all feel better after some food and a good cigar."

Fitzsimmons did not sleep well at his hotel that night. This is so ridiculous he kept telling himself. The north has been tightening the noose on slavery for years. Why shouldn't they? Their economy doesn't depend on slave labor. The South has been threatening secession ever since the tariffs were enacted. It has always been an empty threat, and they have always called our bluff. Is it really so different this time? He wasn't sure. But when he thought of the actions he had taken–moving his assets out of the country-shipping Fitz away–he knew that, whether or not it was different this time, his instincts had taken over and directed some very difficult and lasting decisions.

No. There can be no doubt, if the free state people have their way, and Lincoln is elected, the South will secede. War will come.

It had been a night of tossing and turning. In the lobby the following morning Hubert Daxalt was waiting for him. Hubert, owner of the Island Belle, had offered him a ride home from the meeting.

"I really appreciate this, Hubert," he said, climbing into the carriage. "I could have brought a saddle horse. You sure this is no bother?"

"Of course not, Fitz. My God man, I go right by the Manigault, and there's only the two of us! Besides, you saved Jethro from some nasty business. I'm delighted to return the favor."

Hubert was short, chubby, about forty and a fine man. Fitz and Hubert had cooperated on several business ventures and Fitz had always found him to be selflessly cooperative and level headed.

The cobblestone street was noisy beneath the carriage wheels.

"What did you think of the meeting, Fitz?"

Fitz gave a questioning look and heaved his shoulders.

"Yes," Hubert said with a laugh. "My feelings exactly, and I fear their request for a donation caught me at an embarrassing time."

"Me, too," said Fitz. "This was not a very profitable year on the Manigault."

"I know what you mean. Let me ask you again. I have thirty seven hundred acres and a thousand slaves and you have six thousand acres and a hundred and sixty slaves, and you have only one overseer where I have five. How do you do it?"

"Good," Fitz thought, "something to talk about besides a damn war."

"I don't know, Hubert. Perhaps I'm undermanned? How many overseers did you say you have?"

"Five."

"Why five?"

"To keep them working, to keep them from running off, and besides, you have to teach them everything all over every day."

"You mean you don't have Negro gang bosses?"

"It won't work!"

"It works. I have a black gang boss for each of my sections-for the turpentine, for the syrup, for the fields, and for the livestock."

"I wish that would work for me."

"How many stable boys do you have, Hubert?"

"Five."

"And footmen?"

"Three."

"You only need two."

"One may get sick."

"I have one stable boy who is doubling as a footmen. I have one footman who doubles as a stockman."

"My God. How do they get everything done? It takes all five of my boys to do a day's work of one good man.

"It must be pride, Hubert."

"Your pride?"

"No, their pride. Give them some authority and they'll respond."

"They can't be trusted."

"Then you have no choice."

"I have to do something, Fitz. Every year I go deeper and deeper intro debt. I have to do something differently."

"Why don't you bring your head overseer and watch my operation for a few days, Hubert. Maybe what I do won't work for you, but you may get some ideas."

"Why, thank you Fitz. You may have saved my life. I'll do it."
"Good."
"Sophia!" Fitz called to his wife when the carriage stopped. She looked up from her roses she was cutting. "I've asked Hubert to lunch."

She walked over to where the men were standing. She was tall and graceful. Her golden hair, much the color of honey, was cut short. Actually, it was even shorter than her husband's. This had caused quite a stir when her friends had first seen it. It had reinforced her status as something of a rebel. She was an extraordinary horsewoman, and according to Fitz, a hell of a shot. She, her husband, and Jonathan knew she could run the plantation herself if called upon. Fitz hoped she never would have to.

"Hello Hubert." She offered her hand. "How is Grace?"
"Feisty as ever, Sophia. Thank you."
She turned to her husband. "Did young Fitz get off all right?"
"No problem. His accommodations are excellent and the Captain said he would be personally responsible for him."
"I'm glad." She kissed him.

No doubt most if the plantation would miss Fitz, Jr. He was friendly and respectful of all the Negroes. He was not a little stuck-up brat like many white plantation children. The Negroes loved him for that. They would all miss his happy smile and his readiness to pitch in and help. But nobody would miss him more than Jason, not even his parents.

CHAPTER 7

Jason threw himself into his work and within a few weeks, Samson would be saying: "Slow down, boy. You gonna kill yo'self."

Working harder and faster brought more free time. That was when he would bury himself in his Bible, reading more deeply into its wonders than ever before. At that point, God opened another door to Jason.

It was after supper. Fitz and Sophia had retired to the library. "Fitz, Reverend McGinnis was here today."

"And what did our man of God want, besides an invitation to eat?"

"Fitz, really! That never came up. He was telling me that ours is one of the few churches with no Sunday School for the children."

"I know that. A man should teach his own children. Having a Sunday School is shirking your duties."

"What about the Negro children? How can their parents teach them?"

"That's a good point," Fitz said, realizing the pure truth of the statement.

"I've volunteered to teach the children for an hour every Sunday."

"Did you really volunteer or were you coerced?"

"A little of both, I suppose. But I don't mind."

"Are you going to mix the white and the Negro children?"

"Hardly, dear. I'll just teach the Negroes."

On the following Sunday the plans were announced. The age limits for the classes would be six to sixteen. One might suppose Jason would have been upset by this invasion on his few hours of free time on Sunday. He wasn't. He was elated, even though the class would be held at three o'clock in the afternoon, the very middle of his only day off.

That first day there were sixteen in the class. Jason was one of the older boys, so Sophia told him he was to help her. He wasn't sure exactly what she meant, but assumed it would be to keep the classroom clean. Actually, it was not a classroom; it was a large storage room off the stables.

"Now, children, this is your first time in Sunday School and I must confess, mine too." Sophia looked around the room. It was so quiet, you could hear a pin drop. Every child was scrubbed 'til he shone and they were wearing their Sunday best, such as it was.

"But before we go on, you can tell you mamas that you don't have to dress-up for Sunday School. You can wear your everyday clothes. Now where do we start? I suppose I should ask some questions so we can get started in a good place for everyone. I know you've learned some things in church."

Still not a sound, a shuffle, or a cough.

"Does anyone know what the Bible is? If you do, raise your hand and I'll call on you.

No one raised a hand.

"Oh, come now. Ezekiel? Do you know?"

"Hits the Word of God," Ezekiel said in a muffled voice, eyes averted.

"That's right, Ezekiel! Wonderful! And did you know one of the books of the Bible has your name. The book of Ezekiel."

Ezekiel brightened and visibly relaxed. Somehow this new knowledge gave him a sense of importance he had not felt before.

"Alright. Now, the Bible has two parts. There's the Old Testament and the New Testament. Did anybody know that?"

Most of the heads in the room nodded "yes".

The rest of the hour was spent asking very simple questions. To her surprise Sophia learned that the children knew much more than she had imagined. Perhaps their parents had been teaching them after all. When the class ended Jason stayed to put the benches back against the wall.

"I was really gratified, Jason. The children are very bright. Oh, do you know what I means to be gratified, Jason?"

"Yes, ma'am. Gratification—satisfaction, reward, and..." He shut up. "Watch it you dumb nigger," he thought. "You'll mess up for sure."

"Why, Jason. That's right! That's terribly exactly right! How did you know that?"

"Ah, uh, well, ma'am. I reckon Fitz told me."

Sophia looked at him with penetrating eyes and an amused expression. "What else did Fitz tell you, Jason?"

Jason had regained his composure now. "He used to have to 'splain lots of words to me so as I could understand." His dialect had gotten much thicker.

"I don't remember Fitz ever saying a word like gratify." There was a kindness in her voice that was very disarming.

"It musta come up sometime."

"You found my questions to the class extremely elementary, didn't you Jason?"

"Yes ma'am. I reckon. But that was the place to start, sho' nuff."

"So, elementary came up, too?"

"Ah, uh, well. It mus' have."

"Jason, you are extremely bright. You don't have to hide it."

"Yes 'em."

"Jason, what are the Gospels?"

Jason hesitated. Finally, when he had the courage to meet her eyes, he confessed quietly, "Matthew, Mark, Luke, and John." Lying for Jason was so very difficult.

"Have you read Second Corinthians?"

"Yes, ma'am." Jason literally paled as he realized that she had tricked him.

"So, that's what you two were doing all those months. And the Bible he snitched, did he give it to you?"

Jason's heart fell. His shoulders drooped. "Yes, ma'am. I'll get it for you." It felt like the end of the world.

"Now why would you want to get me your Bible? If Fitz gave it to you, it's yours."

"Ma'am?"

"Have you read it all, Jason?"

"Yes, ma'am. More times than I can remember."

"Do you understand it?"

"Most of it. Well, maybe just some of it. There is so much in there. So much in every verse, every line."

"To be sure. You know, Jason, it is a crime to teach a slave to read."

"Yes, ma'am."

"Then you must help me, Jason."

"Help you, ma'am? How?"

"You must help me protect Fitz. It is his crime as well as yours. We mustn't let anyone know this. Well, not yet."

"Oh, I won't tell! Not on Fitz. I'd rather die than hurt Fitz."

"What else did he teach you besides reading?"

"I can write. He taught me 'rithmatic and history and geography and, well, whatever he learned every day he came and taught me."

He couldn't tell whether Sophia was shocked or gratified, but he seemed to detect a certain gleam in her eyes as if she suddenly felt more pride in her own son than she had ever felt before.

"I declare. That boy of mine!" For a moment she teared. "Jason, I will need your help with the class. I mean with the teaching, too."

"You can depend on me, ma'am. I promised Fitz."

"Promised Fitz what, Jason?"

"That I would take care of you even if they freed me."

"Freed you? What are you talking about?"

"Mr. Lincoln, the war, all of that stuff."

"Fitz obviously shared everything with you, Jason, even our private conversations in the house."

"I'm sorry, ma'am."
"Who have you told this?"
"Not nobody! Not even Mama."
"Good. Let's keep this our secret."
"Yes ma'am. I promise. Cross my heart."
"And spit, too, huh?" she smiled.
"Yes ma'am." And he almost spat.

"I'll tell you some more, Jason. If war comes, the men will probably have to go to fight. That will leave me to keep everything going. I'll really will need your help then."

Sophia wondered why she was telling this child this. Why should she confide in him, and how on earth could he possibly be any help. It was a strange feeling, but for a few moments, she had felt of Jason as a surrogate Fitz. She actually wanted to give him a hug. So, she did. Jason stood frozen. He could not fathom the complex emotions that had engulfed the Manigault's mistress.

Jason looked forward to every Sunday. He loved every minute of Sunday School. Each week, he grew bolder and it wasn't long before he was doing most of the teaching. Sophia would get him going and let him spend most of the hour doing all the talking. Sophia was fascinated. It didn't seem to matter what subject she chose, or what part of the Bible she referenced. Even though Jason kept what he was saying simple, she could tell he yearned to go into things more deeply, with more complexity. But with whom could he make such an exchange? Certainly not the children. Actually, he was beyond even Sophia. She could feel it. She could hear it.

She had begun to evaluate her feelings about Jason. She had never before felt motherly toward one of the Negroes. Jason had become a handsome young man. He was lighter than most of the Negroes, as if there may be a white man in his family tree. His features were somewhat sharp. He did not display the wide nose or large lips of Abraham, his father. Perhaps she was captivated by his mind. She found that when he taught, she, as well as the children, was learning things about the Bible. Even when she had just read it, she had not known. Perhaps she was seeking, unconsciously, a substitute for her son, Fitz. Poor little Fitz. He's just a child. He must be terribly lonely and afraid and homesick. She wiped the tears from her eyes that always came when she thought of her son.

Well, regardless of why she felt this way, she wanted to help Jason. His mind was too good to spend its existence cleaning stables.

CHAPTER 8

It was Sunday and they were dressing for church.

"Fitz, I've decided to go to Charleston tomorrow and spend some time with Aunt Catherine," said Sophia.

"Sounds fine, darling. But hold down the shopping. Things are tight right now."

"I'll be back on Thursday. Would you have Samson come for me about noon? That will give us time to eat the mid-day meal before returning. I'd like to be back around five."

"Fine."

Sophia wanted to see her aunt. The dear old lady was in the very best of health, though she was getting on in years. But her real reason was far removed from Aunt Catherine. That's why, on Tuesday morning, she excused herself from Catherine and took a carriage to the Lambo Street Methodist Church. She was received quickly by the Rector.

"Ah, Sophia, what a delight to see you. May I offer you a sherry?"

"It is wonderful to see you, also, Dr. Gainey. No thank you to the sherry."

"Well then, what brings you to Lambo this fine day?"

"I have a favor to discuss with you, Doctor. I won't say 'a favor to ask' because after we discuss it, I may not make the request of you."

"That's somewhat mysterious, dear lady."

"It's about a young man I know."

"Yes?"

"His mind is fascinating. He could well be a genius. His knowledge of the Bible is mind-boggling to me. He's only fifteen. But he could be a seasoned theologian, to listen to him."

"That is fascinating."

"The favor I wish to discuss...Would you be willing to take this young man in, teach him, let him study with you, and perhaps even work with you?"

"I have done that on occasion."

"Of course I would see to his expenses, or tuition, whatever we call it."

"That would be no problem, I'm sure. A few dollars for his board. Naturally he would help us around the church. That helps defray his expenses considerably. Yes, I suppose you might say we are agreed. After all, if the lovely Sophia Manigault recommends him he must surely be very special."

"He is very special, but there is one other thing, Dr. Gainey." She hesitated. "The young man to whom I refer is a Negro."

Dr. Gainey did not answer right away. He rose, placed his hands behind his back, and paced about the room for long moments. Sophia watched him with knowing eyes. She had created turmoil in his Christian breast.

"Sophia...As you know, we Methodists have been very actively engaged in bringing God to the Negroes. We've built several churches for them, spent quite a bit of money, actually. Sophia, what you ask is most unusual."

"This is a most unusual child."

"I am sure. I don't know if I have the time to take an illiterate black boy and..."

"He is not illiterate, Dr. Gainey. He reads as well as I do."

His eyebrows went up.

"How? Who?"

"That is of little importance, Doctor. The important thing is that he is uniquely bright and an extraordinary Bible student and self-taught."

"I don't doubt that he is what you say, but..."

"Don't you understand, Dr. Gainey? God is at work here."

"My dear, you cannot even dream of the ramifications of this. I, the leader of the largest Methodist congregation in the state, tutoring a Negro boy, why who knows..."

Sophia was a woman of action. She began to grow tired of this seeming procrastination. More importantly, she began to grow angry at the possibility that she would fail. "But," she thought, "this is totally unfair of me. I really have no idea of what I am asking."

"Then you answer is no?" She heard herself say.

"I didn't say that. The Negroes do need their own leaders, especially Christian ones. If the slaves are ever freed...And they, as a whole, do love God..."

He paced a few moments more.

"May I have time to pray about this Sophia? It is not a decision to be made quickly."

"Of course, Reverend. I apologize. Perhaps, I did not realize the difficult position I have asked you to assume. But I think I do now."

"Let me pray on it Sophia. If it is God's will, I shall do it."

"I respect you for that, Reverend Gainey. And, I cannot imagine that God would want the mind of this boy mired in ignorance. So, I will trust in God. Will you give me your answer tomorrow?"

"I will give you my answer tomorrow."

"I am staying with Aunt Catherine. However, I shall be glad to come here again tomorrow."

"If you don't mind, I think that will be best."

"Shall we say ten o'clock, then?"

"Yes. Yes, ten will be fine."

"Let me say I'm sorry again for bringing you this burden."

Sophia left. The Reverend Dr. Gainey was no hypocrite. She knew that. He was a fine Christian gentleman, not a pious ass. He would sincerely pray about, and honestly evaluate, her request. Suddenly it occurred to her that only this morning she had thought of all this as something of a lark. She had been, at best, half-hearted.

But during her talk with Dr. Gainey, she had turned adamant that Jason would get this chance. She hoped her attitude had not appeared bullying to Dr. Gainey. No, no of course not. Gainey could not be bullied. She knew him that well. His fear of the ramifications was not for himself. It was the welfare of the church he had in mind. She truly felt sorry for placing him in this dilemma, but only for a moment.

The following morning, at ten sharp, the housekeeper showed Sophia to a chair in Dr. Gainey's study.

"Good morning, Sophia," he said, closing the door behind him. "Would you like that sherry now? I hope you don't mind if I do. It was a difficult night, thanks to you."

"I'm truly sorry."

"I'm not. It was a rewarding night, too."

Sophia said nothing for a moment. "Dr. Gainey, I really am sorry. I should not have burdened you with this. I..."

"It is a burden. This could cost me my position. It could split my church. It could have me disrobed, and...oh...God knows what."

"I don't blame you for refusing."

"But I don't refuse. It is God's will that I do this."

"You know that?"

"Yes."

"For a fact?"

"For a fact."

"But how?"

"Because it is so outrageous. Because it is...I'm sorry...so damned dangerous."

"Then, if it helps, I'll withdraw my request."

"Too late for that. God has spoken to me. Either bring me the boy or I shall be forced to come and kidnap him."

"I'm not sure I can bring him."

"What?"

"I haven't discussed this with Fitz."

"You...you...what?

For a moment Sophia wanted to laugh, then she wanted to cry.

"You put me through this on a hypothetical basis?"

"No, don't worry Dr. Gainey. I will bring him, somehow."

"Good. You know, Sophia, I am ashamed of myself. When you asked me to do this, all I thought about were the risks, the possible injury to me and to my church. We would all be in terrible trouble if our Lord and Savior had thought that way. They nailed him to a cross. They can only run me out of town on a rail. Bring the boy, Sophia. Bring the boy. Oh, this is a condition. He has to be a free man."

CHAPTER 9

When Samson stopped the carriage in front of the Manigault house, Fitz was just arriving on horseback with Jonathan. They dismounted. Jonathan led the horses away after tipping his hat to Sophia.

"How's Aunt Catherine, darling?"

"Energetic, and as opinionated as ever."

Fitz laughed.

"Walk with me, darling," Sophia said. "I need to get the kinks out, and I want to talk."

"Oh? Sounds serious."

They locked arms and started toward the dock across the large, lush lawn.

"I saw Dr. Gainey while I was in Charleston."

"Is the good Reverend well?"

"Oh, yes."

"Good."

"Fitz..." Then silence.

"What is it, Sophia?"

Fitz, this is difficult for me. I know we're short handed, but Fitz, I need a favor."

"Then ask it."

She took a deep breath. "Fitz, I want you to free Jason."

"Who?"

"Jason."

"What are you talking about?" Fitz had become flushed.

"Jason Apelligo, Meta's boy. I want you to free him."

"Sophia, what in God's name are you talking about? Free Jason? He's just a child. He's..."

"I'll explain if you'll give me a chance."

"He'd starve to death. He'd..."

Fitz! Will you let me explain?"

"I...I'm sorry, dear. Of course, go ahead."

"Alright, but first, everything I tell you is our secret."

"I don't know..."

"Promise?"

He hesitated and looked out across the river.

"Please, Fitz."

"Alright. I promise. But you know I hate to give my word before I know why."

"And you won't get upset."

"Now, come on Sophia..."

"Please."

"Oh, alright. My God, what have you and Catherine cooked up this time?"

"Catherine knows nothing about this."

"That may help. So, tell me."

"Jason can read."

"He can? How in the world?"

"That son of yours. He's been teaching him for years."

"My God. I knew they were close, but it never occurred to me. Little Fitz taught him, huh?" Then Fitz laughed in spite of himself. But his face grew serious again quickly. "That's a crime."

"Just hear me out. Jason has been helping me teach Sunday School. He has read the Bible through and through."

"That's amazing!"

"The amazing thing," Sophia continued, "is that he is a genius. He truly is."

"That's no reason to free him. He can't make it, Sophia. He..."

"Dr. Gainey has agreed to take Jason in and teach him and work with him."

"To what end?"

"Don't you see, Fitz? We have the beginnings of a great Negro leader in our very own stable boy. I've heard you say a hundred times the Negroes can't make it if they're ever freed. And lack of leadership is one of the primary reasons."

"That's true."

"Fitz, I feel like we are part of something very big here. Perhaps it is even divinely inspired. I don't know. But if you could have seen Dr. Gainey this morning..."

"He has to be freed?"

"Dr. Gainey's only condition is that he be a free man."

"He will have no money."

"Yes, he will. I'll pay his expenses."

"No, that won't be necessary. I'll find a way." She didn't notice, nor did he, that he had consented.

"I insist. I know we are financially tight at the moment. I'll use some of my inheritance for this."

"This is awfully fast, Sophia. Have you thought about Meta and Abraham? They will have feelings about this."

"But, surely their feelings could only be positive. Their son will be receiving an education. Perhaps even a career."

"We can't speak for them."

"I'll talk to them, Fitz. It will be alright."

"Well, of course they have nothing to say in the matter. They're my niggers."

"Fitz! How dare you! You know I hate that word...and that attitude."

Fitz laughed. "And you know I do too."

She laughed. "You did sound just like white trash."

Abraham and Meta were overjoyed when Sophia talked to them. Of course, she didn't tell them everything; only that Jason was to be freed and that he would be taken care of and taught by a great man in Charleston. She did reassure them that Jason could visit them as he wished or when his schedule permitted. After all, he would be a free man.

The following morning, Hambone was brought from the stock barns and reinstalled as footman and stable boy. Jason moved back to his mama and daddy's house and awaited his next job assignment.

"I reckon I did a real bad job, Mama. I'm sorry. I tried. I really did." Jason's heart was broken. No one had told him the good news yet.

"Don't feel bad, Jason. You did a good job. The mistress just has you another job...an even better one."

"What, mama? House nigger already? I'm too young to be a house nigger."

"Just you wait. She'll tell you in good time."

Jason took advantage of his leisure time. He studied his Bible, but his leisure did not last long.

He was arranging the benches for Sunday School that Sunday when Sophia arrived early.

"Jason, are any of the others here yet?"

"No, ma'am, it's still early."

"Jason, tonight I want you to pack all your things, everything. Tomorrow, we're going to Charleston. You're going to school there."

"Ma'am?"

"I've arranged for you to go to school in Charleston."

"Me? But I'm a nigger, ma'am. Niggers can't go to school."

"Well, it isn't really a school, Jason. You're going to work at a church and the minister there is going to teach you."

It was slowly sinking in. "You're going to send me to go to school...me...you're going to..." The tears ran freely. He giggled. He cried. "Me, going to school...just like Fitz."

"Not quite like Fitz, Jason. Dr. Gainey will teach you the Bible. And, knowing Dr. Gainey, you'll probably get into the classics and an awful lot of good common sense."

"Classics? What are they?"

"Don't worry, you'll learn soon enough."

The following morning, for the second time in his young life, Jason was seated inside the richly appointed carriage.

Sophia looked down at his "luggage". It was a bundle wrapped with homespun cloth.

"What do you have in there Jason?"

Jason dutifully untied the knot and showed her the contents. There was a shirt (normally washed every other night), a pair of pants (well worn), his Bible, and the slightly worse-for-wear jack knife. He was wearing his Sunday best, including his shoes.

"That's it?"

"Yes, ma'am. These are everything I own in this world."

"I see." She called up to the driver. "Samson, when we reach the city, go directly to Lamar's."

Samson tipped his hat. "Yass'um."

Then she reached inside her purse and extracted an envelope.

"Jason, do you know what these are?"

"No, ma'am."

She took one of the sheets of paper from the envelope and handed it to him. "Read that to me."

Jason opened the paper. It was filled with beautiful penmanship, many capital letters with flourishes. Before he began to read, it occurred to him that he did not write very well at all.

He read: "Know ye, all men, by these presents that I, Fitzsimmons Manigault, do herby on this day declare the bearer, one Jason Appelligo, to be a free man, obligated to no man or institution. Any doubt as to the authenticity of this document may be allayed by the records duly filed and maintained in the court house of Charleston county in the city of Charleston in the sovereign state of South Carolina."

It was signed, of course, by Fitz senior and affixed with a beautiful seal.

Jason could not really grasp what was happening. He did not yet know what it meant to be a slave, how could he feel the impact of being free?

He uttered a quiet "Thank you, ma'am."

Sophia understood. His reaction was as she expected.

CHAPTER 10

"Lamar's" was the finest men's shop in all of Charleston. Fitz, Sr. and Fitz, Jr. bought all of their clothes there, so Sophia was well known by the clerks.

"Mrs. Manigault! Good Afternoon. How may we help you today?" asked Mr. Lamar, the illustrious owner.

Sophia pointed to Jason.

Is he bothering you Mrs. Manigault? Get out nigger! What do you think you're doing in my shop! Get out this instant!"

Jason, wide-eyed, stepped back.

"Mr. Lamar! Please!" Sophia grabbed the store owner's arm.

"This, Mr. Lamar, is Jason Apelligo. He is a freeman and my friend. It is he I wish fitted."

Lamar's eyes widened. "I beg your pardon, dear lady, but this is extraordinary!" He stopped, squared his shoulders and looked at Sophia.

"Madam, I doubt I have anything in the shop that will fit him."

"Sophia's eyes shot daggers. "Then I doubt you will ever again have anything to fit a Manigault, Mr. Lamar, nor a Daxault, or Johnson, or Middleton, or Lambeau, or McGill, or..." her voice was rising. She stopped and stared in his eyes.

Lamar was no fool. Sophia Manigault could well accomplish that if she wished. He could be ruined.

"Perhaps I can fit him...in the back. Please follow me."

Sophia knew they were being hustled out of the sight of any

customers who might wander in. But that was alright, Jason needed the clothes. She hated the thought that, free man or not, Jason had just been introduced to the world in which he would probably have to spend the rest of his life.

Samson and Hambone carried the many packages into the parsonage while Sophia and Jason followed the housekeeper to the church to find Dr. Gainey. He was in the church office.

Jason liked Dr. Gainey almost immediately. He used his very best English, his very best enunciation. Dr. Gainey was impressed, especially when he asked Jason several Biblical questions and Jason responded with chapter and verse, and word-for-word quote

"I must say, Sophia, you were quite right. I am truly excited!"

"Here are the papers, Dr. Gainey." She handed him the envelope. "And Jason, you keep this one in your Bible with you."

"In his Bible, Sophia? He needs to keep it on his person at all times."

"His Bible is on his person at all times, Dr. Gainey."

"Oh," the reverend laughed.

"Mrs. Manly!" The minister called through the door for his housekeeper.

"Sir?"

"Please show Jason to his room and help him get settled in. I'll see you at supper, Jason."

They left to find Jason's new living quarters.

"Dr. Gainey, I have here my draft for one hundred dollars if you'll let me know when that's running low, I will send you another hundred. I would prefer to do it that way if it is satisfactory."

"Quite satisfactory, Sophia."

"Then I must get back. May I visit with Jason from time to time?"

"Surely. I encourage it. I want you to watch his progress."

"I want you to know, Dr. Gainey, I fully appreciate the position I have placed you in by bringing Jason here."

"I won't deny it, Sophia. I have the feeling that soon I will be stoned to death on King Street. But the truth is, it is not your doing, my dear. It is God's. Now, what kind of Christian would I be if I did not respond to the will of God?"

"I'll pray for you Doctor."

"Please do, dear lady. Please do."

CHAPTER 11

Fitz's, Jr.'s trip to England had been the longest, dullest, most depression-filled interlude of his life. A fifteen-year-old boy accustomed to hunting, fishing, running and playing over vast stretches of farmland and forest had not taken well to such cramped quarters. Homesickness, and a gnawing fear of the unknown, had not helped.

As the ship docked and he looked around him, there was little to brighten his mood. The London waterfront was filthy, ancient, and rotting. It was littered with trash. All round him were rough-looking men who were so dirty their body odor was almost visible. There was tremendous hustle and bustle that raised a din of unintelligible noise.

There was one bright spot. A beautiful carriage with two magnificent, spirited horses stood waiting. Standing beside the carriage, a tall and handsome man, obviously a gentleman, waved to him. He dispatched his two footmen up the gangplank to fetch Fitz's trunks. He followed them up, cane in hand.

"Fitz?" His voice was strong and his penetrating eyes danced with friendliness.

"Cousin Monty?"

Monty extended his hand. "By God, you look just like Sophia!" It's good to see you, my boy. How was your trip? No, never mind. We'll talk in the carriage.

"Captain, a job well done. Our thanks for looking after the boy."

The captain touched his index finger to his cap. "My pleasure, Lord Hastings. I think you'll find we took good care of the young master."

Fitz gave his thanks and in minutes the carriage was winding through the narrow streets away from the wharf.

"Now then, Fitz, tell me. Is everyone well?"

"Yes, thank you, Cousin Monty."

"You know, you were only two the last time I saw you. Do you remember my visit?"

"I'm not sure, sir. I may remember it or, perhaps, I remember Mama talking about it."

"I remember it well. Your parents were such gracious hosts! It's my pleasure to return the favor."

"Are we going directly to the school, sir?"

"No, we are going home, that is, to my home. You'll be staying with me."

"But...I thought it was a boarding school." Fitz felt a strange sense of relief. He hoped he didn't sound as if he were protesting.

"It is a boarding school. Your father has heard rumors of hazing in our English schools and he would have none of that. Frankly, it's true. The boys do get rather severe. I made arrangements for you to be a day student. Are you disappointed?"

"Oh, no sir. I didn't mean to infer that. I was, well, I was dreading staying there."

"Well it wasn't easy. The headmaster finally honored my request and allowed it. I don't live far from the school, so commuting will present no problem. You have a tremendous amount of adjusting to do, Fitz. We will help you in every way we can."

"Thank you, sir, I'm sure. I don't even know what questions to ask."

"No need for that now. No hurry, really. You don't start school for three weeks yet. You can spend that time resting and getting accustomed to things."

Hastings House was breathtaking. A large country home, even larger than Manigault House, it was situated on rolling hills less than a mile from Creighton Hall, the school that awaited Fitz. One mile in the opposite direction was the small, picturesque village of Kenton Vale.

As the carriage stopped in front of the house, Monty said, "I see William is putting on a show for you."

Fitz had noticed the line of people as the carriage was approaching. It was the household staff. He was introduced to each of them in turn. The men bowed, the women curtsied. Only one name did he remember–Mary, the upstairs maid. She was small, with hair and eyes as black as night. There was a sensuousness about her smile that made his fledgling hormones bounce from his heels to the top of his head. For a split second, all the stress of anticipation he had felt for weeks left him. A feeling of warmth, and a slight tickle in his stomach, replaced all reality.

His room was no less beautiful and comfortable than the rest of the house.

By dinner that evening, Fitz had grown far more comfortable with his surroundings and with his cousin. He realized that Cousin Monty was rich. Monty was a relatively young man, probably even younger than Fitz's father.

"Papa tells me you are a banker, Cousin Monty."

"Yes, Fitz, I am. By the way, why don't we drop the cousin and just call me Monty."

"Thank you, sir. I will."

"And we can drop the sir also. You and I are to be great friends, Fitz."

"Thank you, Monty. That does sound strange though, considering everybody else is calling you "Lord" and that stuff."

Monty laughed.

"Fitz, had you been born here you would be a Lord, too, just like your father would have been."

"Really?'

"Really. If you'd like, we'll have everyone refer to you as Lord Fitz."

"Thank you, no, please."

"You know, Fitz, I've been quite impressed with you. You are extremely well spoken for your age. You are obviously very bright."

"I've had some good teachers."

"I'm sure. Certainly your father agrees with me. You and I will jointly manage his investments while you're here. Oh, yes, I am to keep you informed of all transactions. Your father wants you to be fully aware of all his holdings in the event of...in any event.

"In what event, Monty?"

Lord Hastings' eyes grew serious as he examined his wine closely. "Events in America are taking a nasty turn, Fitz. There is much talk of rebellion in the South, and it would appear there is more to it than just talk. Promises have been made. If this man Lincoln is elected, your South Carolina has stated, emphatically, that it will secede. The national leadership has stated, just as emphatically, that will not be allowed. Even if it means war."

Fitz already knew all this.

"They have said that many times, Monty. Papa said secession has been an empty threat ever since the tariffs were passed."

"But this time is different, Fitz."

"Did papa say that?"

"No, but you are here, aren't you? And so is his money."

As the days passed Fitz learned the house, and the village, and began to feel very much at home. He rapidly became a favorite of the servants who went out of their way to be kind to him. They were not accustomed to the straightforward brash honesty of an American teenager.

Liking Fitz was very easy, but with only one of them did Fitz concentrate on being liked. That was Mary. Fitz would carefully plan "accidental" meetings with Mary around the house. Sometimes in the kitchen, sometimes in the hall, but mostly he would "stumble" upon her working in his room.

"You sure do keep it clean in here, Mary."

"Tis my job, Master Fitz."

"I know, but you do it so well."

Talking with Mary was not easy. The tickle in his belly was distracting. He usually kept the chance meeting short.

Then, one morning, Fitz awoke ill.

"It's just a nasty attack of hay fever, my Lord. Keep him abed, warm, and lots of liquids. I'm sure he'll be fine."

"You hear the Doctor, Fitz?"

"Yes, sir."

"You'll take your meals in bed for a few days. No running about, now. School begins next week. William, see to it, won't you?"

"Yes, my Lord. Leave the young master to us. We'll have him fit shortly." The butler bowed ceremoniously.

The following morning, after the breakfast tray had been removed, Fitz was half asleep when the latch of his bedroom door clicked. He turned his head to see Mary tiptoeing into the room.

"Oh, Master Fitz, forgive me. I did not mean to waken you."

"It's alright. I wasn't really asleep." Fitz felt the tickle again.

"I can straighten up a bit later."

"No, now is fine."

"You're sure, now?"

"Yes."

He watched her as she moved around the room dusting, straightening. Her uniform fit her snugly, smoothly clinging to the curves of her body. Occasionally, when she straightened and her breast heaved proudly, he could feel his breath catch. He was almost sure she could feel his eyes and read his thoughts, so he decided to make conversation.

"What does the staff think of me, Mary?"

"Surely now, you're not concerned with the feelings of the servants." He could detect a bit of playfulness in her voice.

"Of course I am. I like you all very much."

"And they like you, Master Fitz. They admire the plain spoken honesty and friendliness of you Americans."

"And you Mary? Do you like me?"

"Now is that a fair question to be asking of a poor working girl?"

"Poor?"

"Well, compared to you..."

"I'm not rich."

"Oh? Rumor has it that Lord Hastings has invested more than a million pounds sterling for you."

"Not for me. For my father."

"Same thing."

"A million? Are you sure?"

"Well, now. I said is was a rumor. I shouldn't be talking so with the young master."

"I'm not young. I'm as old as you."

"You're fifteen and I'm sixteen, a grown woman."

"I'm going to be sixteen!"

"I must say you are mature for your age." She continued her dusting, a little more than necessary, Fitz thought. He could feel his groin begin to ache.

"You know I could lose my job for being familiar."

"Don't worry. I need someone to talk to. Can't it be you?"

"When school begins, you'll have lots of hoity-toity friends, Master Fitz."

"I wish you wouldn't call me that. Call me Fitz. We American's are not so formal as you British."

"Well, now, I am British, you know, and I'm not of the peerage."

I don't care. You are nice, and...and very beautiful," he ventured.

She stopped and looked at him for a long moment.

"Shall I make your bed? You could sit over there."

"I think not, I..."

"Oh, come now, it will be much more comfortable." She grabbed his hand and pulled him up. Her touch electrified his entire body, and when the covers fell away his excitement was evident.

"Here now!" She stared, and a grin danced across her lips. "We'll have none of that!'

Fitz retreated to the easy chair, red as a beet. She hurriedly straightened the bed and started out the door. As she opened it, she paused, turned, and with an impish grin on her face said: "I do believe you are going on sixteen. You Americans mature early...and rather well." With that, she closed the door and was gone.

Fitz wasn't sure, but he thought he might have been complimented. He no longer felt embarrassment. Actually, he felt elated. There had been something about her eyes, her smile, the toss of her head that held promise. The pressure he felt was terrible. He climbed back into his bed, and with fantasies of Mary, relieved it.

CHAPTER 12

The day before classes were to begin, Monty introduced Fitz to the Headmaster who gave him a tour of the school. In the process, he met his professors and several of his classmates. Everyone was exceedingly friendly and helpful. Fitz was beginning to learn that people would be nice to the ward of their Lord Hastings. It did not hurt that Monty owned Hastings House, most of the village, and all the lands for miles around, and the parcel of land on which the school was situated. That information Fitz learned from Mary who was becoming friendlier, and easier to talk with every day.

"Because of who you are, Fitz, your father and I feel your education should be in business and in law. You're going to need to know how to handle a vast fortune someday. Knowing accounting, management, that sort of thing, is a must, and too, being conversant with the law is an absolute necessity. I'm afraid I've rather prescribed your studies to the Headmaster."

"That's fine, Monty."

"Then you don't object to my having selected your curriculum?"

"Not at all."

Thus Fitz was launched into the English academic world. It came as a shock to him. He had been accustomed to a soft spoken, easy going tutor for three to four hours per day. His tutor had been understanding, coaxing, and forgiving. Not so with his new professors. They spat facts and figures as fast as he could write. They demanded immense amounts of reading, writing, and research. They were strictly business. He had feared his classmates would be cold to him, or at least resentful. That was not the case. There was no time. They were as overwhelmed as he. Perhaps, had he lived in the dormitory, it would have been different. He decided he would never know.

He was able to find a few free hours on the weekends. That saved his sanity.

At the Christmas break, Monty visited the Headmaster.

"I am delighted to see you, Lord Hastings, especially in light of the excellent report I have."

"Then Fitz is doing well?"

"Extraordinary! He's at the top of his class. He is truly a brilliant young man."

"Good. I had feared the adjustment would detract from his work."

"Apparently not. His professors, to a man, have discussed accelerating him."

"Do you think that wise?"

"Not at the moment, no. Perhaps at the end of next semester."

That evening Monty discussed the meeting with Fitz.

"I say, Fitz, you do make us proud!"

"Thank you, Monty. I was just trying to hang on."

"Well, hang on you have."

"Are you going into the city again tomorrow, Monty?"

"I'm afraid so, Fitz. A banker has to keep a high profile, you know. Don't want to be suspected of absconding with funds." They both laughed.

"I hoped we could go riding. I haven't ridden since I left home and I do miss it."

"No reason you can't go, this countryside is perfectly safe. And I'll wager you're a good horseman."

The following morning the stable boy brought King Henry out, saddled and ready.

"He's a fine horse, Master Fitz. A bit spirited, but gentle enough.

If you get lost, just give him his head. He'll come home straight away."

The English countryside was beautiful. The air was clean and crisp. The powerful animal beneath him gave Fitz a feeling of exhilaration. He rode for miles in a great circle over the rolling meadows, across small streams, and through the many lightly wooded areas. When at last they came upon a small winding trail between the school and Hastings House, Fitz dismounted.

"I'll walk with you a while King Henry. I'm sure this leads back to the house."

"Hello Little Lord and Master Fitzsimmons."

Fitz turned to see two boys from the school. They were older than he.

"Hello," Fitz said. "Are you enjoying your holiday?"

"We are now," said one of them. "How are things back home?"

"Fine, I'm sure."

"Don't you miss beating and starving your slaves?" Fitz felt the hostility.

"We don't beat them or starve them."

"You buggers treat them like animals. Everyone knows that Mr. High and Mighty."

"I'm afraid you are misinformed." Fitz wondered why he said that so formally.

"I'm afraid you are misinformed," one of them parroted with extreme sarcasm. "Lord Big Wig's ward can't stay in the dorm, he may get hurt."

"Oh how frightful," the other chimed in.

"You know what you need Sir Snot? You need to be taken down a peg."

The hair on the back of Fitz's neck bristled.

"If you two want a fight, you're going about it just right."

The larger one parroted again, "If you two want a fight..." and punched Fitz in the face. Fitz went sprawling at the surprise impact. King Henry bolted and disappeared down the trail.

The other boy dove for Fitz, but Fitz rolled to one side and the young man landed flat on the ground. Fitz was on his feet quickly. Left jab, left jab. Blood spurted from the larger boy's nose. A right cross and now the larger bully was sitting flat on his backside. Fitz turned his attention to the other boy just in time to get another fist in the face. The next thing he knew, they were on top of him pounding, pounding. The pain became less sharp. Blackness engulfed him.

"Fitz! Good Lord! Fitz!" He opened his eyes to see Mary's face staring down at him. "Are you alright?"

"My mouth hurts," he mumbled.

"You're a bloody mess! Let me help you up. There's a stream over here. Let's get you cleaned up."

His mouth hurt, but his ribs hurt even more. He could barely stand. He struggled with painful steps. Finally they made the water's edge and Mary helped him sit down on the mossy bank. She tore a strip of cloth from her petticoat, wet it, and gently began to dab his face. He winced.

"How did you find me?"

"The whole bloody staff is scouring the country side. King Henry came home without you. Lord Hastings will be livid with us."

"Why? It's not your fault."

"Perhaps not, but we're charged with your safety. What happened?"

"A couple of boys from the school don't like Yankees."

"Obviously they hate Yankees."

"Mostly slave owners."

"From the looks of your knuckles you made a response," she said as she applied the cool, wet cloth to them.

"Ouch! They hurt too! I hurt everywhere!"

She gently kissed his sore knuckles and then she placed her cool hands on each side of his bruised face and softly kissed his swollen lips. It was obviously his first kiss.

"Now does that make you feel better?"

"Not yet. The rest of my body still hurts. "It is quiet and secluded here. Maybe you can kiss them all better?"

"My God, man. You've had the stuffin' beaten out of you and you're thinkin' o' that. Your beating has made you awfully bold, Master Fitz."

"Uh, huh. If my head were clear, I wouldn't have the nerve to approach you. But, now that I have…"

She dropped the cloth and lowered her eyes.

"You know you can order me. You are the young master, after all. And I need my job…"

Fitz sobered instantly. "Never, Mary. I apologize. If that's the way you think I am, forgive me and let's get back to the house."

She leaned over and kissed him again, this time she instructed him.

"Loosen your lips," she whispered.

He did, and slowly she separated them with hers and let her tongue dart inside them. He grew bold and fumbled to feel her breast. After long moments, she took his hands in hers and moved them away.

"The young master has a lot to learn. But not here, and not now," she whispered.

Then she raised her voice to normal.

"Let's get you home. Everyone is terribly worried. And besides, how can you enjoy kissing with those damaged lips?"

At dinner that evening, Fitz had the soup only.

"My God, Fitz!" said Monty. "Your whole bloody face is swollen shut. Tell me the names of those rough necks."

"If you don't mind, Monty, I'd like to handle this myself. Besides, the Doctor said nothing is broken."

Monty started to protest, but caught himself.

"Very well. I suppose you're right. But if there is a repeat of this. There will be the devil to pay…"

That night the soft, down pillow felt as if it were made of bricks. I hurt now, Fitz thought, but boy, wait 'til tomorrow! He felt exhausted, but sleep would not come.

Sometime, in the small hours of the morning, there was a familiar click and the rustle of the covers as a warm body snuggled in beside him. He did not have to ask who it was. The clean, natural, refreshing aroma that always surrounded her gave her away.

"Mary?" It was not a question.

She said nothing, but put her arms around him and pressed the full length of her body against his. At that instant his pain vanished and his entire being sang with music that emanated from every cell. Then she reached down and touched him. The surprise, the electricity, the feelings...something...! He exploded.

She giggled softly. "Don't worry, you'll be back in a minute."

And he was. The lessons began. Perhaps she knew very little, but it was worlds more than he knew. Together they could learn it all.

CHAPTER 13

Jason worked hard at the church, cleaning, polishing, helping the housekeeper, as well as being the janitor. He studied hard too. Dr. Gainey kept the agreement and directed Jason in his studies two hours per day. He would assign Jason reading. The following day they would spend the two hours discussing, expanding, and theorizing until both were satisfied. Then, the new assignment would be given. They also took meals together. This was an opportunity to learn the social graces and, from time to time, simply to chat. It was at such a time on a Sunday evening that Dr. Gainey said, "You know, Jason, we may, in the final analysis, be doing you a terrible disservice."

"I don't see how, Dr. Gainey."

"Well now, perhaps when we're finished, you may be neither fish nor fowl. On the outside, you'll be a Negro in a white man's world. On the inside, you'll be a white man in a Negro's world. Perhaps you shall never fit anywhere again. I'm serious, my boy."

"I have thought about that, Dr. Gainey. I have thought on that a lot. And, I've prayed about it. I have decided to be a man in God's world."

"My boy, you are mature beyond your years," he sighed. "Would that could that be the case."

"Maybe it can't. But I intend to try. Not just for me, but for everybody."

"Well, to change the subject...I know you've only been here a few months, but I've made arrangements for you to speak at the Negro church on James Island next Sunday."

Jason's eyes widened. "You mean I'm going to preach the sermon?"

"Let's don't call it that. You're far too young. You're going to speak to the congregation."

"On what?"

"We'll think of a topic. Frankly, I would prefer if you prepared it yourself."

"I will, Dr. Gainey, I will."

"You can rehearse it to me. Let's say, oh, this Thursday at lessons."

"May I be excused? I'd like to get started."

"Too excited to eat, huh? Very well. Go, my boy."

Jason retired to his room to work. Dr. Gainey retired to his study to relax. Mrs. Manly, the housekeeper, answered the impatient knock at the door.

"Excuse me, Doctor."

"Yes, Mrs. Manly?"

"Elder Jamison is here to see you."

"Please, show him in."

"Good evening, Bernard," said William Jamison, the church's senior elder and largest contributor and one of the few who addressed the Reverend Doctor by his first name.

"Good evening, Mr. Jamison. Is something wrong?"

"No, nothing. Well, perhaps. I realize this is an awkward time to call, but there's talk..."

"Talk of what?"

"That you have a Negro slave here to whom you are teaching the gospel. But what is worse, reading also."

"That would be breaking the law."

"Precisely. I thought we should clear that up. Such a rumor could make trouble with the congregation. It is a rumor, is it not?"

"Since I have no idea where the information originated, and since it is inaccurate, I would say it could be called a rumor."

"You're talking in riddles, Bernard."

"I am not teaching a slave boy. I am, however, tutoring a Negro freeman. It is for a fee. He is extremely helpful about the church. I am breaking no law. Is that direct enough?"

"Teaching a Negro could be construed as breaking the law."

"No. Teaching a slave to read is what the law states."

"You know very well it is meant to keep the Negro from learning. Educated Negroes mean trouble."

"I understand your concern, Jamison. I assure you I am doing nothing in secret. Certainly, I am doing nothing questionable in the eyes of God. His law, when you get right down to it, is the law I must obey." There was an edge in his voice.

"That's not the point and you know it, Bernard. We are speaking of the real world. Income. A split in the church. Scandal. I am not your enemy, Bernard, nor am I your critic. I am simply executing my responsibilities to the church. We must put an end to his rumor."

Dr. Gainey sighed deeply. "Mr. Jamison, before I assumed the duty of teaching Jason Apelligo, I prayed diligently. I believe, by teaching this bright lad how to minister to his people, I am doing a service to God. The Negroes need ministers. Certainly this is no precedent. I did pay homage to man's law when I made my decision. I required his master to free him prior to any instruction. I want you to know, and I will inform the congregation, I am doing God's work. If that should require my resignation then it shall be so."

"No, Bernard. I think not. We just need to get this thing out in the open. Stop the rumors. I am sure, the way you explain it, that things will be all right. I think I understand and I think our good people will too."

"I'm sure they will. They are good people. Nevertheless, I will not turn back on this."

"Don't corner yourself, Bernard. Just explain it."

Jason had prepared what he considered a very interesting discourse on the Good Samaritan. Dr. Gainey found it informative and well done.

"Your delivery is excellent, Jason. If I didn't know better I should think you were a man of thirty. This will be just fine. Work on your eye contact. By the end of your talk, you should have looked into the eyes of every member of the congregation. Don't speak to all of them. Speak to each of them."

The trip to James Island did not take as long as Jason had hoped. He was nervous, and not sure as to whether it was fear or excitement. He had gone over and over his material in his mind until every word and planned gesture was securely embedded.

Sitting behind the pulpit while the Negro minister preached his sermon, Jason's anticipation grew in leaps and bounds. The butterflies arrived and his knees began to quiver. Finally the Minister said: "We got us a young freeman here today who gonna talk awhile. He's learnin' preachin'. Ya'll listen to what he got to say. This here's Jason Apelligo. He growed up on the Manigault plantation."

Jason stood and walked to the pulpit. He was petrified. He put both hands on the pulpit to steady himself. The silence was almost overwhelming. His knees shook. His breathing was shallow. He did as Dr. Gainey had instructed. He took a deep breath and looked around the sanctuary.

Hundreds of eyes looked back. There were sad eyes; there were hollow eyes; there were hostile eyes.

In that moment the real world rushed into his mind and his soul. "What am I doing?" he thought. These people don't need to hear about the Good Samaritan. They don't need eloquent words and practiced gestures. They won't even understand me.

"My friends. Before you, you see a nigger who ain't know nothin' about livin' compared to you. I ain't got a scar on my body. But you, you have scars on your wrists and ankles from your chains. There's scars on your backs from the whip; your faces from the back of the white man's hand. This is bad, but it ain't the worse. It's the scars inside, they the worse."

The heads began to shake in agreement. Across the sanctuary eyes began to soften.

"I is too young to tell you anything 'bout livin'."

"Thass right," shouted a man in the back row.

"I is too young to tell you 'bout dying."

"Thass right," echoed from several places around the room.

"But I has read my Bible!"

"Sho nuff.. Sho nuff."

"And I gone tell you what the Bible say. Not what I say, 'cause I don't know nothing! What the Bible say, the Bible is what knows!"

"Amen."

"Amen."

"Amen."

"It's yo' body what heals itself from the scars of the whip. It's you body what heals the scars from the chains."

"Yassa."

"That's right."

"Amen."

"But only one Almighty God in Heaven can heal the scars inside."

"Glory."

"Hallelujah."

"Only God Almighty can take them away, but he needs your help. Jesus Christ never said nothin' 'bout no slaves. He wouldn't talk about it. I reckon he hated the thought of it."

"Thass right."

Praise the Lord."

"But Paul did. Paul say slave, obey yo' master. But he also say master, be good to yo' slave! Don't beat up on him! Feed him good! Keep him warm!"

The entire congregation was participating now, caught up in the fervor that Jason was feeling.

"What is it that all this mean? Really, once you think about it hard, look at it close, what do it mean?"

There was a silence.

"Nobody can make you a slave! They can chain your body. They can starve your body. They can strip the hide of yo' bones, but they can't git inside and make you a slave! God is inside there! You think the white man can whip up on God? Let me tell you, it's God who gonna whip up on the white man."

Silence. Perhaps even shock.

"Now if you ain't got God inside of you, then you is a slave! But if God is inside you, no amount of whipping gonna make you a slave!" Jason's voice continued to rise. You a freeman 'cause God got yo' soul, not no white man! Turn to God! Give him your soul, and all the chains and whips in the world will not enslave you..." The air was electric. Jason looked from face to face, "Amen."

You could hear a pin drop.

On the trip home Jason was troubled. He had hoped for a better reaction. He had pictured himself as winning the congregation, having them love and admire him, think he was wonderful. The Negro preacher had looked at him with disbelief.

"Don't you stir 'roun' in my congregation no mo', boy!"

To say the least, Jason was confused. 'Stir in my congregation.' Had he done that? He had only said that the love and acceptance of God was the only truly freeing experience. At least, that's what he had meant to say. Could they have misunderstood him? More likely he had simply not communicated properly.

CHAPTER 14

"How did it go, Jason?" Dr. Gainey asked that evening at dinner.

Jason was staring into his plate. "I'm not sure, Doctor."

"Hmmm. Perhaps the good Samaritan is beyond them yet."

Jason hesitated, then looked up. "I didn't do my prepared talk, Doctor Gainey."

"Oh? Well now. What did you do?"

"I tried to tell them that the only true freedom in this world is found in the love of God."

"Then you spoke on freedom?"

"Well, no sir. I spoke on the love of God. I just, sort of, told them that was the way to be truly free...regardless of their chains, so to speak."

"Jason, that could be very dangerous subject matter, in view of the times and so forth. How did they react to you?"

"They didn't. They just sat there in shock."

"Dear me."

"I didn't intend to shock them, Doctor. It's just that, well, when I looked at them, the good Samaritan seemed so nieve, so terribly, I don't know, inappropriate."

Dr. Gainey's eyes widened.

"Perhaps I'm not making myself very clear."

"Perhaps not. Tell me, Jason, is it your intention to be a Minister of God? Or is it your intention to be a rabble rouser?"

"A man of God, sir."

"Good."

"However, I'm beginning to see that this is open to considerable interpretation. If the rabble are God's people and they are being victimized..."

"Slavery is wrong, Jason. There is no interpretation needed on that."

"I know, Doctor."

"It's just that it's so complicated any more. Freeing them under the wrong circumstances, without proper training, without careful preparation, could be a very un-Christian thing to do."

"Yes, sir."

"On the other hand, we are remiss. We should have begun the process long, long ago. The economy has trapped us. In spite of the totally miserable wrongness of slavery, it is also a terribly inefficient way to run a plantation. Yet our landowners are trapped. They have the tiger by the tail. If they let it go it will consume them. If they hang on, in the end, it will consume them."

"I suppose it is much easier to intellectualize the problem, Doctor. If we look at it from the stand point of Christianity we are seeing a doomed society."

"Isn't that what I said?"

"Well, yes sir. I suppose it is. But to me this is not an intellectual exercise. These are my people."

"And you see yourself as a modern day Moses, don't you Jason?"

"Moses saw himself as an inept man being terribly pressured by his conscience, and God, to help his people. I, too, am inept. And, yes, I'm going to do what I can."

"Then be careful. Talks such as you made today must be thoroughly thought out, or they'll hang you for sedition."

Jason almost jumped.

"You know more than I thought, Dr. Gainey."

"I know all about it. The minister is petrified, but I think there is no need for worry. Chances are good that it will end there. And then you are so young. Next time say what we rehearsed."

"I'm not sure I can promise to do that."

"Jason, damn it boy! You must not ever say anything that people can construe as trouble making. When you talk to your people, it must be on sweet Bible stories. It must be on the rewards of servitude. They must understand that they will receive their happiness in the next life by behaving in this one."

Jason could feel anger rising inside his chest.

"You never said anything like that before, Doctor," he spat the word 'Doctor'.

"You never gave me cause."

"It was not my intent to create a problem, but..."

"I know. And I don't think anything will come of it."

"But, if I have to create problems to help my people, I will!"

"What do you mean?"

"Doctor, I can't believe you are preparing me to preach in order to keep my people docile."

I...I...well, it's just that it never has been the way of ministering to the Negro."

"But I want to bring them the true Word of God, and the true dignity of man."

"My God, Boy! What have I been saying?"

"You've been saying "Preach to keep them in line. Preach but don't make trouble."

"I have. I really have. God forgive me!" I really have!"

"Then I can do as I think right next time?"

"No! My child, you are too idealistic, too head strong. I don't want you hanging from a tree. No, I want you to be honest, but we must be careful. Not that I will help you teach rebellion, mind you. But I do reserve the right of censorship while you are under my supervision."

"But..."

"Don't' get too big for your breeches yet, Jason. I mean what I say! You only have to worry about yourself. I have a church, a congregation, you, and my own career to consider."

"Doctor, I know I've got a lot to learn, but this double standard you're talking about, I..."

"You're right. You have a lot to learn. A very lot. Why don't you go to bed Jason. We don't seem to be communicating very well this evening. Good night."

Good night, Doctor."

During a night of tossing and turning, Jason began to have an inkling of what his mentor was trying to tell him. A man of God was stretched many ways in these times. There was a responsibility to bring the Word of God to the people–all of the people. But survival in your position, even your life itself, depended upon paying homage to the morays of the society. Yet, this was hypocritical. Jesus would not have stood for this; he would have done the right thing regardless of the consequences. But we are not Jesus. If we are foolish we will accomplish nothing. Survival must be considered. Somehow we must survive and preach the truth. But how? How can one walk such a tight line? And how can one who serves two masters ever accomplish anything? It was a troubled and sleepless night.

The next meeting the elders held was disastrous. Jamison had not been nearly so understanding as he had led the Doctor to believe. Prior to the meeting, he had done his work. He had contacted each elder individually and made his point.

"So, Dr. Gainey, the opinion of the elders is unanimous. This boy must go." Jamison said it with finality.

Dr. Gainey stood before them in shock. He had not even been afforded the opportunity to present his case.

"Can't we discuss this, gentlemen?

"I'm afraid the vote has been taken. Further discussion is out of order." Jamison crossed his arms.

"I see. Then my feelings, and the facts, are not to be considered?"

"Your 'ward's' talk on James Island was scandalous, to say the least. We cannot afford to be associated with a loud mouthed trouble making nigger."

"He's a child with the most brilliant mind I have ever known. He speaks the English language as well as I. He knows his Bible better than I. He..."

"The vote has been taken."

"Then I shall have to consider my response."

"Be careful, Doctor. Don't be foolish. You are not held to accountability...yet."

"I shall consider my response and give it to you in the next three days." Gainey left the room, a most unusual behavior on his part.

CHAPTER 15

Jason, dejected, packed his possessions. Three suits, two pair of boots, six shirts. So many clothes, he thought.

Dr. Gainey entered the room.

"Jason, I shall accompany you to the Manigault plantation. I have much to explain to the lady of the house."

"Yes, sir. I'm ready." There were tears in his voice. He picked up his jack knife and carefully tucked it into his pocket. Then lastly, and most importantly, he clutched his Bible to his heart.

In the carriage Jason said, "I'm sorry, Doctor. It happened so fast, I don't really know what I did. I..."

"You did nothing so terribly wrong, Jason. They simply found the ammunition they needed."

"My talk."

"I'm afraid so. But think of it this way. It was not for naught. Somehow, no matter how small, you have already made an impact. You had to, or the reaction would not have been so strong."

"But I've gotten you into a lot of trouble, too."

"Nonsense. My trouble stems from the fact that I wish to serve God, not man."

"Listen, Doctor. Is that thunder?"

The Doctor listened.

"Driver! Stop!"

The carriage pulled to the side of the road. Gainey listened.

"It's cannon, Jason. It is the roar of cannon!"

Then they noticed the commotion all about them as it grew in intensity. People were riding, walking, even running, toward the Battery, a point between the junction of the Ashley and Cooper rivers where Charleston's defenses had been concentrated.

"What is it, Doctor?"

"I fear it is the beginning of the end, Jason. Driver! Proceed!"

"Aren't we going to go back and find out what's happening?"

"What is happening will be with us for sometime to come. It can wait."

Jason sat patiently in the foyer of Manigault while his mentor and his ex-mistress talked in the library.

"You messed up, boy!" It was his father, Abraham.

"Yas suh." His English lapsed.

"You some dumb niggah, you know dat? Freed! A chance for a education. An' you go an mess up!"

"Leave the boy be, Abraham." It was Meta. She took him in her arms. "He's just a chile. He doin' the bes' he can." Jason cried softly, staining the highly starched sleeve of her uniform.

Inside the library, Dr. Gainey continued his explanation.

"It is just that we are not ready for someone like Jason. He is a powerful threat, though I doubt anyone knows how much of a threat he really is; at least, not yet.

"I understand, Doctor Gainey. This presents me with a terrible problem. I hate to see his mind go to waste. I don't know what to do."

"You could have sent him north, I suppose. But I am afraid that is now out of the question. The cannon were sounding when we left Charleston. I fear the war has begun."

Sophia's eyes widened. "I knew it was coming, but already? You present me with many problems today, Doctor. Fitz is the commander of the local regiment, you know."

"Yes."

"Dear God. What's to become of us." It was not a question. It was a lament.

"Well, dear lady, as for myself, I am leaving Charleston."

"Why?" Sophia was surprised.

"It seems the only way I can protest the elders' decision. I am resigning Sunday during the service. And when I finish with what I have to say, there will be no tuning back."

"Don't do this for us, Doctor."

"Madam, I do this for myself."

When she said good-bye to Dr. Gainey, Sophia turned to Jason. But before she could say a word, Fitz came rushing from the back of the house.

"Sophia, come help me pack. I have to be in Charleston tonight."

"Why? What's happening?"

"My God. It wasn't bad enough that they took Fort Sumter. That was enough to start this thing. Now, that damn fool Beauregard is bombarding a Federal ship. This is bound to bring the Yankees down on us. My regiment has been ordered to Charleston to dig in and to repel an invasion."

"But it has been over three months since they took the Fort. It will be weeks before they react..."

"And we need weeks to prepare. I'm taking Hambone with me as my orderly. You'll need to replace him in the stable."

"I'll have to use Jason."

"Jason?"

"He's back."

"But you can't use Jason. He's a freeman, remember?"

"I just can't think right now. Don't worry, I'll take care of it."

"What's he doing back?"

"That can wait, Fitz."

"Alright, I have to hurry."

They left the foyer and went up the stairs. Jason looked around the room, and sighed deeply. He went to the kitchen.

"Mama, I'm goin' to the stable. I guess I'll be in the hayloft."

CHAPTER 16

Life on the plantation had not changed at all since Jason left for Charleston. Every dirty little routine job was still there to be done, day after day. And as the weeks passed, there was still little change. Fitzsimmons' Manigault came home often. His regiment was entrenched around Charleston, but not one Yankee had appeared. It was all getting rather boring for the troops.

Jason, too, was getting bored. He felt his talents were being wasted. He began to change.

"Jason, you dumb niggah. Ah tole you to clean dat stable yestiddy!" Samson roared.

"Don't scream at me you stupid niggah." Jason's frustration overcame him. "I'm a freeman. You ask me nice or I'll have your black hide stripped right off you. You understand me, you old stupid fool? I'm a freeman. Do you understand? Do you?" Jason shook his fist in the old black man's face.

Samson's mouth fell open. He had no idea what to do; so he went to find Jonathan.

"Samson, he's right. He has been freed. Everything he does is out of the goodness of his heart. He's not getting paid, at least, not to my knowledge. But, I'll talk to him," Jonathan said. "After all, we still have to operate this place."

And he did.

"Jason, it's not that we don't understand," Jonathan said. "But Samson has to run the stable as he sees fit. Now, if you can't accept that you should talk to Mrs. Manigault. After all, you are eating her food."

Jason was livid, but he constrained himself. Softly, he said, "I'm as free as you are, Mr. Mitchell. I resent being treated like a common niggah around here. Samson is stupid, yet he is over me. I resent that."

"Perhaps so." Jonathan was losing his patience and an edge came to his voice. "I have to respect the fact you are free, boy, but I have a plantation to run. I'll have to personally run you off the Manigault if you give me any more trouble. Now, do you understand that, Mr. Free Black Boy?"

Jason turned and walked away. He would speak to the mistress, he decided.

Sophia was in the library going over the books. Her brow was furrowed. Jason opened the door and walked in. She looked up.

"Jason? Why didn't Abraham announce you? Worse yet, why didn't you knock?" Her reception, or actually the lack of it, surprised him.

"I'm sorry, ma'am. Maybe I should come back later."

She leaned back in her chair and rubbed her eyes.

"What is it?"

He realized she was very tired. For a moment his problem seemed rather insignificant.

"I wanted to talk to you about working in the stables," he half mumbled.

"What? I didn't hear you."

"I'm not happy working in the stable."

There was a long moment of silence while Sophia tried to compose herself and not allow the anger that arose in her to burst out.

"Go on, Jason."

"I just don't think it's right to have a freeman working for an old slave... and not pay him either."

Silence again. Sophia wanted to come out of her chair and scream at this little upstart; this little thankless upstart to whom she had been so unbelievably kind. But she continued to hold herself in check.

"Things have been rather hectic for me. I understand. But you must admit, Jason, your situation is rather, ah, unusual."

"I am capable of better things than cleaning up after a horse."

She began to lose her grip on her temper.

"Well, young man, I'm sorry we don't have the Presidency to offer you or its accompanying twenty-five thousand dollar salary."

Now it was Jason's turn to be silent. He felt his temper flair. It was a feeling that he had not yet become accustomed.

"I ain't gonna work for no niggah."

Sophia bounced from her chair. Leaning forward she said: "You will work for whomever I choose or you'll get off the Manigault." Then Sophia, in spite of herself, lost her temper. All the pressure had come to bear on one focal point. "You miserable, thankless...Do you know how much I have spent on you in the last several months? It would take you fifty years to earn it. Now the Manigault needs your help and you...you. Who...what are you, Jason? What happened to you? Where...?"

Silence again. She straightened and began pacing. She was tired. She was frightened. Now she felt betrayed by a boy she had showered with concern and money. Perhaps if she were in a better mood, she could be more understanding, or not at all understanding. She didn't know.

"I'll talk to you about this tomorrow. That is, unless you choose to leave Manigault tonight." She wished she had not said that.

Jason felt as if he had been struck in the face. He never dreamed she would be anything but completely concerned about him, but she had practically ordered him off the plantation. His self-importance had gotten out of hand and his timing had been poor. But he did not yet know how poor. He excused himself and returned to his unlighted, drafty hayloft. He was hurt. He was angry. He was confused. He had, too soon and too completely, become the center of the universe. He had become self-centered and self-serving. He did not know it. He never would. Then he remembered Fitz's last words: "Take care of Mama and Daddy." He felt shame in his heart. His hopelessness and his frustration had driven him to become somebody he did not even know; someone he did not like.

CHAPTER 17

In the house Sophia continued to pace. Fitz's regiment had been ordered north. Lee had decided there was no threat to Charleston and was building an army in the Manassas area. With Fitz in Charleston, running the Manigault plantation had been one thing, but with him so far away, she felt the full impact of her loneliness. Then she looked at her desk, at the account books. They were terribly short of money and so many mouths to feed. It was not a good time to give her yet another problem.

When the sun rose on the Manigault the following morning, it also rose on the moods of Sophia and Jason. Things did not look so hopeless in the light of day. What Sophia had said to Jason did not fall on deaf ears. During the night, he had realized that Sophia considered him prepaid and expected some of the concern she had shown him to come back to her in her hour of need. She had cast her bread upon the water. Sophia began to see that Jason had been given a taste of living in relative luxury, and more importantly, dignity. She could understand this difficulty in giving that up. Yet they had both been hurt by the attitude of the other.

Abraham went to the stables.

"Boy, the Mussus want to see you. Wash yo' hands and come on."

Sophia was having coffee on the porch. It was a beautiful sunny day. The silver service sparkled from the rays reflected by a million droplets of dew that covered the lawn like diamonds.

"Yes, ma'am." Jason held his hat in his hand, hoping the gesture would help him apologize.

"Jason, I've been thinking about our conversation last night." She did not invite him to sit. "I think I understand. First, you are a free man under no obligation to me or the Manigault. You may leave anytime you wish and no one will try to stop you. Second, I cannot afford to pay you. If you stay, you must work. You can sleep at the stable and eat in the kitchen. That's the best I can do. I'm sorry, but that is the way it is."

She was all business. There was no motherly concern seeping through her attitude as in the past.

"I'm sorry ma'am. I owe a lot to you and the Manigault, and to Master Fitz. I would like to stay, and I promise I won't get the bighead again."

"If you stay, you know you will have to take orders from Samson."

"Yes, Ma'am."

"Very well. You may stay."

"Thank you, ma'am," he said in a subdued manner, but he was hurt by the "may". He turned to leave.

"One more thing, Jason."

"Yes, Ma'am?"

"Never, and I mean never, come to me again unannounced."

He winced. "Yes, ma'am."

When he returned to the stable, Samson was waiting.

"Well, is you gon' work?"

"Yes," Jason answered.

Samson laughed. "I recken fo all yo' uppidy-up egication yo' belly done won out." He laughed again.

But it was not his belly that had changed him. It was his almost forgotten promise to Fitz. I won't let my pride dictate to me again, he thought. Not ever!

CHAPTER 18

Fitz had begun riding at every opportunity. He enjoyed it. He was also determined that this beating would not scare him into staying within the safe confines of the estate. He rode almost every day, but particularly on Mary's day off. They would meet by the stream where she had found him that day, and make love on the moss-covered bank. They had become proficient with practice. No more pawing or panic. No more premature ejaculations.

They were in love. Each day Mary grew more beautiful as her legs lengthened and her hips and breasts rounded. Fitz's shoulders broadened. His voice began to take on a deep resonance, and once a week he shaved.

"When I finish school, Mary, we'll be married. Then I'll take you home to America to the Manigault. You'll love my mother. She, too, is a beautiful lady."

Mary snuggled closer in his arms. "But I am no lady, Fitz."

"Maybe not in England, but in America you are. In my heart you are." Then he kissed her.

"How will we be able to go? The war...

Fitz sighed deeply. "I know. And there may be nothing to go to. But I have the money. We will rebuild if necessary."

That evening Fitz and Monty held their monthly meeting concerning the Manigault's investments.

"Things are unbelievably splendid, Fitz. Your net worth has grown thirty percent since you father transferred his money to England."

Fitz was studying the tally sheets. "I can see that, Monty. It would appear that this one, Liverpool Ironworks, is mostly the reason."

"It is, Fitz. We show a profit there of almost forty percent in the last seven months. That's truly remarkable."

"What do they do to make them so successful?"

"The make cannons. Their production has more than quadrupled since the Americans began placing orders with them. And, of course, their profits are exorbitant."

"The Americans? The North or the South?"

"Both, actually. Unfortunately they can't ship the South's orders. The blockade, you know."

"You mean the South's cannons are paid for, but not delivered?"

"Some of them are. Blockade runner, a privateer here and there. But it's difficult."

"Something is very wrong here, Monty. I'm making a profit from cannons that may be raking my homeland."

"Someone will make the profit, Fitz. It may as well be you."

"Don't you understand? I don't want to profit from a gun that may kill my father or blow up the Manigault house. I'm sorry, Monty. This is wrong of us."

"Fitz, we're not buying Yankee cannon. We're taking Yankee money. We're not giving them anything."

"Yes, but it just seems like something is not right about it. I feel like a, well, a parasite, even a traitor."

Monty thought for a long moment. "Alright, Fitz. If you like, we'll pull out of the iron works, however, I advise against it."

Fitz smiled. "No, I have something better in mind. How much have we made off the iron works?"

"Give me a moment. Ah, close to a hundred thousand pounds."

"And how much for a blockade runner?"

"I haven't the foggiest. I would suspect ten thousand pounds or so."

"Monty, I want to know how many cannon the South has unshipped, and how many blockade runners we would need."

"Now just wait a minute, Fitz. I can't spend you father's money like that."

"You said it was a joint effort between the two of us."

"That's on investment decisions, not spending the profits."

"For God's sake, Monty. My father may be under fire at this very minute without a single cannon to help him! The responsibility for this is mine. I assume it all! Now please, do as I ask."

Monty sighed. "When you put it that way..."

"Please."

The boy is right, he thought. If things go badly, by God, if things go badly, I'll replace the money. It can be my contribution."

"Very well, Fitz. I will."

It took two months to hire three ships at the rate of eight thousand pounds each. One of them made it into Charleston harbor. One went down in a storm. The third was blown from the water by a Federal gunboat. It took six months from his decision until he heard the results of the ships he had dispatched. The iron works' profit replaced the money Fitz had spent. So he did it again. Meanwhile, his other investments grew also. On the second try both ships that were dispatched made it and returned with cargos of cotton. Fitz's profits greatly exceeded his costs.

"Well, how about that, Fitz? Your patriotic gesture has created a profit." Monty laughed.

"I know. So this time, we buy the ships as well as transport the cannon. Monty, my friend, we're going to build a shipping line."

And they did. But had Fitz known, it would have been better to ship food and clothing. People all over the South were hungry and poorly clothed. Well-fed, well-equipped, fresh Federal troops swarmed into the South in overwhelming numbers. The North's manufacturing power and large population were too much for the tired, brave men who faced them. Port Royal, uncomfortably close to Charleston, had long since fallen. The first attacks on Charleston itself had been beaten back, but the war of attrition was taking its toll. It was just a matter of time, and time was with the North. Each day they grew stronger. Each day the South grew weaker, hungrier, more depleted in every way. Southern armies, decimated by endless fighting and forced marches and by lack of supplies and equipment, could no longer win with daring and fortitude. More and more often Northern armies marched forward unopposed. They raped, burned, pillaged and murdered with abandon, much as the Great Khans centuries before had done when the world was still, justifiably, uncivilized. But, of course, this was Yankee "strategy".

The Manigault was not spared. First it was the Southern army. On a dreary rainy day, a contingent of cavalry came tearing up the oak lined approach. The captain in command wheeled to a stop at the house while his troops dispersed across the plantation. Sophia met him at the door.

"Ma'am, I'm Captain Gilchrist of the 23rd," he saluted.

"Yes, Captain?"

He handed her a crumpled document.

"This is a requisition signed by General Huntly. Our troops are starving, Ma'am. We'll be taking the live stock and any stored grain you may have."

Sophia's face fell.

"I understand, Captain. But in God's name, I have close to a thousand people to feed. Surely you won't take everything."

"I'm sorry, Ma'am. I've got twenty-six thousand hungry troops. All I can find will never be enough."

Sophia protested, but in the end, they took every cow, horse, chicken and pig. There was one exception. The sergeant who entered the stable looked at the beautifully matched pair of carriage horses and said: "Don't take them boys. They ain't no good for riding and they too purty to eat."

When the Captain presented Sophia with the receipt and inventory of what they were taking, he said: "The Confederate States of America will reimburse you, Ma'am, just as soon as the war is won."

Sophia took the receipt. She said nothing.

"Ma'am, the Yankees ain't far. I recommend that if you've got any valuables, you hide 'em somewhere. They're stealing everything."

Sophia went back into the house and sat down. Shock?

Depression? She was ready to give up, to end the worry; to stop the fight. She sat quietly for a long time. She gazed around the room with sad eyes. "This will soon be only a memory," she thought. "This house, my things, all that we have worked for will only be a memory."

Then her eyes grew hard. She threw her shoulders back and held her head up.

"Abraham!"

"Yass Ma'am?"

"Get Mr. Mtichell. Then you and Meta and the rest of the help start gathering the silver and china. Bring it all in here, everything worth anything-the candelabras, the paintings, everything!"

When Jonathan arrived, Sophia explained her plan.

"We'd best pack them in hog's heads, Ma'am. We'll tar them on the outside for water proofing."

"Good. They won't be buried long. But they must be protected."

Everything Sophia considered precious, irreplaceable or expensive was frantically, though carefully, packed in the huge barrels and loaded on the largest wagon they had.

"Thank God they left two horses," Jonathan said. "I'd hate to have to back pack this."

By dark they were ready.

"Samson, you and Jason will come with me." Jonathan said. "Get three shovels."

Under cover of darkness they pulled away from the house. They went by the edge of the river for a while, and then swung into the forest. They stopped by "Big Sally". That was what they called the tallest pine on the Manigault. Jonathan took fifty steps due south from the big tree.

"Here," he said. "We have to dig a hole the size of that wagon. So we better get to it. The night was quiet; the ground was soft. Jason felt like every muscle in his body was dissolving. By daybreak they had refilled the hole, scraped the loose dirt, and scattered the leaves. In a few days, one would never know a treasure was buried there.

CHAPTER 19

"It's done, Ma'am," Jonathan said to Sophia when they returned.
He told her the exact location. "Only the four of us know where it is."

"That's alright. I trust the four of us. Now, how do we feed ourselves today, Jonathan?"

"Just as we discussed, Ma'am. The teams start at daylight."

Ten men went squirrel, rabbit, and bird hunting. Twenty women went fishing. Twenty more men and women searched for roots, berries, and gleaned the sweet potato field. By late afternoon, everyone ate something.

"We'll pool our findings in the stable every day by three o'clock," Jonathan ordered. "You may as well plan on one meal a day unless you're under twelve years old. The children eat twice.

Nobody complained. Once a day was more than most in the south were eating.

For many days the new routine went well. The gleanings were fewer each day, but the hunters and fisherwomen were lucky. Every day everybody ate stew. It was cooked up in huge washpots with everything they had managed to find thrown in–squirrel, rabbit, sweet potatoes, an occasional 'possum, day lily roots, berries–whatever was brought in. It was filling. Sophia and Jonathan knew that soon the gleaning would be completely depleted. They needed to do something more.

After the meal on the third day, Sophia rose and spoke to her people.

"I cannot ask you all to stay here and starve to death. I don't know if there is any food left in all of the South. But if there is, and if you want to try and find it, you're free to go. Those who wish to leave, just go to the porch. I'll write out your papers."

She rose and went to the house to get pen, paper, and seal ready. There was silence.

After a few minutes, Hosea, a young buck of about twenty, rose and started for the porch. As he passed, Big Mambo reached out, jerked him from his feet and threw him back to where he had been sitting.

"Missy need us, niggah!" he hissed. That was more words than he had spoken in years.

"No, Mambo." Jonathan stepped forward. "Missy meant what she said. If you want to leave, it's alright. She'll free you and let you go. It's alright."

He helped Hosea to his feet and pushed him toward the porch where Sophia was waiting. In all, about a hundred of them lined up at the porch. They were mostly young men and women, several of them with their children. As they received their papers, they went immediately to their huts and packed their things. Without exception, they turned toward Charleston. They thought of it as some legendary place. A place synonymous in their mind with a bright future.

The older ones shook their heads. The wisdom of their years told them there was nothing out there but hardship. Even more hardship than on the Manigault. Jason, too, shook his head. Those people had never been on their own. They worked hard, yes, but someone had always been there to look after them, to think for them. They would not get along well. He hoped they would, at least, somehow survive.

That evening Jonathan reorganized his hunting, fishing, and gleaning groups. He started two of the men making traps for fish and for small animals.

"Whatever you can catch will help. But no rats," he told them. "Not yet, anyway," he whispered as an afterthought.

In the next few weeks, the road passing the Manigault became a major thoroughfare. Hundreds of people were moving both ways. There were hundreds coming from Charleston who had found nothing there. Soldiers of both sides, North and South, could be seen moving in both directions. The Northern troops were cavalry, shining, clean, energetic. The Southern troops were stragglers, almost always struggling on crutches. They were bandaged and bloody. It was pure chaos.

Big Mambo and a dozen other men were stationed at the head of the avenue to keep people out. There was nothing on the Manigault for the refugees, but that did not keep scores of them from slipping across the fields, into the barns, to rummage for themselves. Fights broke out constantly between the Manigault people and the intruders. Jonathan was kept busy dashing from one point to another restoring order. It was difficult to be angry with the refugees. They were starving. They took everything, anything, they could carry in the unlikely event they could trade it for food.

"We can't protect everything," Jonathan told Sophia. "We can protect the house, but we'll have to forfeit the rest. Let them help themselves to whatever they want."

Sophia was in shock. She had been for days. She looked at him with vacant eyes. "Do whatever you think is right, Jonathan. I don't care anymore."

Over the past few weeks, she had freed hundreds more of her slaves who wanted to leave and find something better in that mysterious world out there beyond the Manigault. There were fewer than a hundred of them now. They were mostly old or children. Only Mambo and the fifteen or twenty he had intimidated were strong enough to defend the Manigault. And, of those, only Mambo could be trusted to stand and fight. But fight what? Desperate, starving people, hysterical with fear? Mothers of children whose bellies had begun to swell? There was really nothing to protect, nothing to save, nothing to hope for. Sophia sat on the porch and hoped somehow she would awaken to find this all a nightmare. But, of course, she did not.

Jason had been assigned to look after the children. He made them as comfortable as he could in the hayloft of the stables. He made sure they each had their share at mealtime. He told them Bible stories. He comforted them when they awoke, crying in the night. Everyone felt helpless, but all did what they could for the others.

CHAPTER 20

Long expected, it was a bleak day for them all when the contingent of Yankee cavalry arrived. The Major in charge was extremely polite to Sophia.

"I regret, Major, that I cannot offer you a glass of sherry," she said in her most dignified voice. "But, as you can see, the house has been looted of practically everything that could be carried," she lied.

"That is unfortunate, Mrs. Manigault. But, as the General is fond of saying, "war is Hell.""

"Particularly for the vanquished, Major."

"And the man of the house? Where is he?"

"The last I heard, Colonel Manigault was moving his regiment to the Augusta area."

"I see. Well, to business. I have been ordered to requisition Manigault house for a temporary headquarters. You and your people will have to move out. We need every room."

"I am afraid not. I cannot allow you…"

"Allow, lady?"

"Of course. This is my home. You have no right…"

"Madam, you have no "rights". I can, and will, do what is necessary to follow my orders. That includes executing those who stand in my way."

"Then perhaps you will have to." Sophia was petrified with fear, but she maintained her presence.

"Don't be foolish, Mrs. Manigault. I am a humane man. There are advantages here."

"Advantages?"

"Of course. Cooperate and we may not burn the house. Give us no problems and I'll allow you and your people to eat with my troops. At this moment, Madam, the most you can hope for is to feed your belly and, just maybe, save your house."

Sophia sat down. She had no choice. She decided to cooperate. Not to aid and abet, but to cooperate. It would be useless to do otherwise.

"Very well. We shall give you no trouble."

"Splendid."

⋅⟨⁘⟩⋅⟨⁘⟩⋅⟨⁘⟩⋅

The headquarters contingent left as quickly as it had come. Sophia stood in the rose garden and watched as wagon after wagon pulled out, laden with her possessions. The piano, tables and chairs, sideboards, fine lamps, even window hangings. When she looked inside, she saw the scuffmarks on the floors, broken bottles, shattered plaster. Everything was broken, even her heart. Nothing was left but an occasional broken mirror or shattered chair.

"Get out lady, she's gonna burn!" shouted a Union sergeant.

"You can't burn my home. The Major said you would leave it standing!"

"Not according to my orders."

"Wait, wait. Where is the Major?"

"He's around somewhere. Awright boys, git the coal oil," he yelled. Then he whispered to Sophia, "Try to talk the Major out of it. Sometimes he don't burn 'em."

She found him out front, mounting his horse.

"Major! You promised me! No trouble and you'd leave the house alone."

He looked down at her amused.

"I said maybe."

"You made it clear. As far as I am concerned you gave me your word as an officer."

He simply shook his head from side to side and grinned.

"Are you saying the word of a Union officer is worthless?"

The grin faded.

"Are you enjoying this Major? Making war on women and children?"

"I don't make war on women and children, only on the enemy."

"And I am your enemy? This house? Those children in the stables? Are they also your enemy? You're a lucky man, Major. Your enemy can't fight back!"

The Sergeant stood on the porch, torch in hand, waiting for the Major's nod. The Major looked at Sophia, then the Sergeant. Then he turned in his saddle to see some of the children coming around the house.

"Mount up, Sergeant. We've a long way to go."

Then he looked up at Sophia, saluted, wheeled and led his troops through the oaks at full gallop. In moments, complete silence descended upon Manigault house. Only the birds raised their voices. Everyone seemed to stand frozen in time. Then, slowly, they began to move around. Jonathan came to his senses first.

"Mambo! Get your people to their positions. Meta! How's the food supply?"

"Them Yankees left some grain, some salt pork and some coffee, but not much Mr. Mitchell."

"Alright. Hunting parties, fishers, gleaners, get on with it. Trappers, check your traps. Let's try to get ahead a little bit."

"Praise God," Meta cried.

"What is it?"

"They didn't find the salt. A whole sack."

The two horses were still in their stalls. Samson had been devoting his life to them. They were all he had left. He looked at them with tears in his eyes. They were a reminder of the good times. A painful reminder. Jonathan came into the stable.

"Massa, dey needs some grain. Dey ain't had nuttin' but hay way too long."

"No grain, Samson. There is none to spare. But try to keep them healthy. We may be eating them."

Samson teared up. He knew it could come to that.

The days turned into a week, the weeks into a month. The small game was disappearing at an alarming rate. The gleanings had become nil. Even the fishing was poor. The few supplies the Yankee troops had left behind were long gone. It could not become more hopeless.

"We're going to have to eat the horses, Samson," Jonathan said one evening. But before we do, we must get Mrs. Manigault to safety. Tomorrow at daybreak, have the carriage ready. We'll take her to her Aunt Catherine in Charleston."

"Yass suh."

Sophia was completely demoralized, in no condition to protest. Jonathan helped her into the carriage. Then he, Mambo and Samson mounted the carriage. They took Sophia away from her beloved Manigault house. She looked back as they rode away through eyes that had not shone, except with tears, for a long, long time.

The trip to Charleston was beyond Jonathan's most foreboding misgivings. They had been on the road two hours and were still three hours from Charleston. The road was rutted deeply from the Yankee cannon that rumbled over it in seemingly unending numbers. The refugees blocked their way. All along both sides of the road, refugees and Southern wounded soldiers lay dying. They pleaded for help from the rich man's carriage. Twice Mambo and Jonathan had to beat back desperate men and women trying to hitch a ride. Then they were forced off the road by a battery of artillery in full gallop. The carriage axel snapped like a twig. The horses, rearing, became tangled, fell, and the carriage rolled over on its side. No one was hurt. They gathered themselves and accessed damaged.

"We'll have to walk," Jonathan said.

"We should go back," Sophia replied.

"No. We will get you there if it's the last thing we do."

From the direction of Charleston, there was another rumble of horsemen. Jonathan looked up, expecting cavalry, but it was not.

"Renegades!" Jonathan shouted. "Get into the woods. Now!"

But it was too late. They were pulling up in front of them.

"Well now. If it ain't the Manigault bunch," the leader said.

There were a dozen of them. Dirty, unkempt, unshaven, vile men. They were heavily armed.

"We don't want trouble," Jonathan said in a strong, calm voice.

"Mr. Overseer, you don't know what trouble is."

Jonathan had a glimmer of recognition.

"This here is Bobby T. Don't you remember me?"

"Vaguely," Jonathan said with a cutting edge in his voice.

"I see you got yo' big nigga with you. Watch him, boys. He's bad with that ax."

There were several clicks as rifles and pistols were cocked.

"Just take your blood suckers and move on. We have nothing with us worth taking."

"Well now, the lady looks like a whole night of entertainment to me. Fetch her Simons!"

One of the men dismounted and reached for Sophia. His outstretched arm suddenly fell to the ground. Mambo's ax had severed it with a whistle. Mambo's head exploded as two rifle balls entered it. His chest spurted blood as three more balls tore into him. Jonathan pulled his revolver and blew two men out of their saddles before a pistol shot tore his throat out. Then two of the men dismounted and beat Samson to death with their gunstocks. Bobby T. pulled Sophia across his saddle. They spurred their horses, leaving their armless friend to bleed to death along the side of the road. The refugees, walking along the road, barely looked up. No one stopped. No one could have helped anyway. They continued, zombie-like, plodding to nowhere.

CHAPTER 21

By the following morning, Jason and the others were losing hope that Jonathan would return. They felt the two whites, their only hope for survival, had abandoned them. By mid day, the remaining young bucks, angered by Jonathan's abandoning them, and with no Mambo to stop them, slipped into the woods and disappeared. Only Jason, his parents, and a few very old and very young remained.

"Papa," Jason said to Abraham. "You got to take charge."

At that moment, in a small wooded area not far away, Sophia's ravaged body lay crumpled on the ground. Her severed jugular methodically pumping her life back into the earth from which it had sprung.

As the days passed and no one returned, the seventeen blacks remaining on the Manigault moved into the house. They brought in hay and made beds. The children played throughout the mansion, defecating and urinating wherever it was convenient. The older ones followed suit. They cooked what they could find in the marble fireplaces and threw whatever was inedible on the floor. Someone decided there could be treasure hidden in the walls or behind a secret panel somewhere. Everyone, but Jason, began tearing at the plaster in likely areas throughout the house. They tore up flooring, ripped out the cherry wood paneling, and tore bookcases from the wall. But, of course, they found nothing. The more they found nothing, the harder they searched.

"Jason," Abraham said. "They's talk in the road you can buy food in Charleston iffen you got Yankee money or somethin' to trade. You help bury the silva. We can sell dat for food."

"It ain't ours to sell, Papa."

"We's starving, boy. It ain't doin' nobody no good buried in the groun'. The Missus don't care if we 'live or dead. It would serve her right."

"But how we gonna git it to Charleston?"

"I don't know, but we's gotta do somethin'. Dey ain't no treasure in dis house. We done near tore it apart."

"Papa, if we dig up the silver and stuff, somebody's gonna take it from us. We can't get it to Charleston. Even if we could, we couldn't get the food back here."

"We got to do somethin', boy."

That evening, just before dinner, a familiar figure turned through the gate and walked slowly toward the house. Meta was looking through the window when he came close enough to be recognized.

"Hambone! It's Hambone, ya'll. The Massa comin' home. Praise God, we gonna be saved!"

Everyone ran into the yard, excited and happy. Only then did they realize Hambone was alone. Without even saying hello, or welcoming him home, Meta asked the question that everyone wanted answered.

"Where de Massa? He comin' on?"

Hambone, filthy, tired, hungry, simply burst into tears.

"Oh my Lord!" Meta cried, and burst into tears also.

"De Massa dead," Hambone said just above a whisper. "De Yankees, dey kill him near Columbia. Dat been a week ago. I'se been comin' home ever since."

Everyone fell silent. Hope that ran so high only moments before was now totally gone.

"I is so hungry," Hambone moaned.

"They's some 'possum stew in de house, Hambone. Come on."

They sat silently while Hambone gorged himself on the stew. They said nothing when he vomited it up, went back, tried again, and vomited again. Finally he gave it up. He sat down heavily and laid his head back against the wall.

"I seen Mambo, Samson, and Mista Mitchul on de road back a ways. I thinks it was them. They was wid de carriage. Who killed em?"

"Who killed 'em?" Jason jumped up. "You mean they dead?"

"Been a couple of days, I'd say."

Jason's heart fell. "The lady. She dead too?"

"The lady? I ain't seed her."

"Maybe dey was comin' back, Jason," Abraham said. "Maybe she safe at Mrs. Catherine's."

"De carriage wuz pointed towards Charleston," Hambone said.

"Could of turned 'round, Meta said. "Wuz de hosses dere?'

"No, weren't no hosses."

"Damn!" said one of the old blacks. "I wuz countin' on eatin' dem."

"Hush up," cried Meta. "You ole fool!" Everybody dead and you thinkin' 'bout nuttin' but yo belly!"

"My belly is all I got lef to think about!"

Another week passed. There was almost nothing to eat. Hambone developed a fever and, before long lapsed into unconsciousness and died. He was just too tired and malnourished to fight. After they buried him, Jason knew something had to be done. It could not be put off any longer.

Jason said to Abraham, "Papa, I'm nineteen years old. I'm taking charge."

Abraham was too demoralized to object.

Jason turned to the group. "Git what you want to take, we're going to Charleston."

Jason knew that if Sophia was with Catherine she would help them. If she was not, perhaps Mrs. Manly was still housekeeper for the church's minister. Maybe she would help. Maybe the church would. Nothing was certain, except that they could not remain on the Manigault and hope to survive. They were too old, and too young, to help themselves. So they started for Charleston. They left in a single, demoralized line. Mattie watched them from an open window. Old Mattie, the mid-wife, would not leave her beloved Manigault, no matter what. No one noticed that she wasn't with them. They had to stop every fifteen or twenty minutes to let the old ones rest. The young rested too. They were all weak, undernourished. Whatever possessions some of them had bundled up and brought along were soon stripped away by passersby looking for food. Jason's jack knife was securely tucked into his pocket. The Bible was safe enough. No one could eat it and no one could probably read it either.

They should have been in Charleston by dark. But when the sun set, they were less than half way there. Jason picked a small wooded area a hundred yards off the road for them to spend the night. It was late April, but the temperature still fell near freezing. It was a long night. The rising sun was a welcome sight. But two of the old ones did not wake up.

"Jed and Carrie both dead, you dumb nigga!" Abraham said angrily. "I lets you be in charge and you kills both Jed and Carrie!"

"They were old, Papa, and weak. They died from being run down, hungry and cold."

"Dumb niggah." Abraham turned and walked away.

Jason knew his father had to blame someone. How much more could they take? So much dying. So much hunger. So much nothing left. So much fear of tomorrow.

They started for Charleston again. The going was even slower, more difficult. By mid-day another of the old ones died. She just sat down during one of the breaks and quietly drifted away. Abraham looked at Jason with more condemnation in his eyes. By mid-afternoon, they realized that Jed and Carrie's three grandchildren were missing. With Jed and Carrie dead, they had gone unaccounted for. The rest of the day was spent trying to find them, but they never did.

They were so close to Charleston, they could almost smell it. But they had no choice but to spend another night in the open. They were twelve very cold, hungry and tired people. Papa Jo died that night.

"Seems like I done as much diggin' as walkin' the las' few days," Abraham said at the graveside. "I hopes I never has to dig another grave with my fingers an' a stick."

They were in pain from hunger as they slowly moved into the edge of Charleston. Most stumbled along from weakness. Jason wanted to double up from the gripe in his gut, but held himself erect. They were a pitiful group, but no more pitiful than most they had passed.

Then they smelled food cooking. It was then they noticed that off the road, once again in a wooded area, were hundreds of Negroes. There were campfires, and there were wagons moving in and around the area. Jason thought for a moment it might be some sort of carnival that Fitz had once described to him. Then a tall stately old lady walked briskly toward him.

"Jason? Is that you boy?"

It was Aunt Catherine!

"Yes, ma'am," Jason said smiling broadly. It's me. It's all of us from the Manigault. Jason looked around searchingly. Where's Mrs. Sophia?"

"Mrs. Sophia?" I haven't seen her."

"But she went to see you a week ago."

"Oh, dear Lord. I haven't seen her!"

At that moment one of the old blacks fainted, crumpling to the ground.

"My goodness. Is he ill?" She went over to help him. Jason went to him. He was still alive.

"No ma'am. We haven't eaten for days. He's weak."

"Then let's get you fed! That's why I'm here, bringing food."

Within the hour, they were eating soup. It wasn't good, but it was hot and filling. Catherine had been talking to Jason like a magpie. She had asked him a hundred questions. He answered them all, but did not mention what Hambone had seen.

"I am worried to death about Sophia. Where on earth can she be?"

Jason just shrugged, not daring to meet her eyes, not yet.

"Have you heard from Fitz, Sr.? They say his regiment was near Augusta."

"I'm sorry ma'am," he paused for a long moment, not realizing the fear that was rising in her. "He's dead."

"On, no!"

"Yes, ma'am."

"But how could you possibly know that? It can't be true."

"His man came home without him. He told us."

"Where is he? I want to talk to him!"

"He's dead, ma'am. He died the week after he got home."

Catherine stopped talking. She put her head in her hands and silently wept for a long time. Finally she held her head up.

"How many Manigault people do you have with you, Jason?"

"Countin' me, and if no more have died, eleven."

"Eleven out of so many?"

"The lady freed a lot of them. Some ran off. Some died."

"I don't know what's to become of us, Jason. I don't know if I can look after eleven. I've spent practically everything I have to help feed these poor people. I was so counting on Fitz and Sophia!" She burst into tears again, but quickly wiped her eyes and stood, head held high.

"Enough of this, as soon as they are fed, we will go to my house. Don't worry young man. Old Katie isn't licked yet. Not be a damned long shot!"

May and June passed. The Negroes were comfortable in the carriage house behind Catherine's home. But Jason knew they could not remain and eat day in and day out indefinitely. He watched as Catherine sold almost everything of value to buy food. The food prices were outrageous. What she received for her linens, silver, and family heirlooms was a pittance compared to their real value. But the market was flooded with the once proud possessions of Southern ladies and gentlemen.

Meta had assumed control of the kitchen and made every potato and carrot count. Abraham ran the sparsely furnished house on Gadsen Street with the dignity and efficiency it had come to deserve. Every inch of the small, almost non-existent yard was planted in vegetables. Food supplies, clothing, and other necessities had begun arriving from the North, but they all seemed to wind up on the black market at unbelievable prices.

Jason wandered the streets of Charleston daily, looking for any odd job he could find and any idea he could think of to help the situation.

CHAPTER 22

Charleston had taken a pounding from the Federal fleet. There were many buildings that had been burned or blasted away. Some were completely gone. Some were partially standing and deserted. One such building was the Lambol Street Methodist Church. At first Jason stared in horror at the ruins of the magnificent building. For a moment he stood frozen. Then he walked into the ruins. The sanctuary was completely charred by the fire that had almost gutted it and half of the roof was gone. The rest was dangerously close to collapsing. Miraculously, the parsonage next door was undamaged. Jason knocked at the door. It opened.

"Yes? Jason!" It was Mrs. Manly.

"Yes ma'am."

She invited him in, thrilled to see a familiar face. She shared her meal with him. Shrimp and greens.

"My nephew caught the shrimp. He gave them to me. The greens too. I'd have starved to death without him. He has a boat, you know. Oh, a little one, but he can fish and shrimp. He sells them too." She went on and on. "I haven't seen Dr. Gainey since the week after you left. He was such a kind man. And dedicated to the Lord. They broke his heart, they did. God told him to help you and the elders wouldn't allow it. He had to leave, poor man. His commitment, you know."

Jason felt guilty. All this time, all this hardship, and he had become so intent on his problems that he had barely even thought of

God. No wonder things had been so difficult. He had all but turned his back on God. He was at least guilty of ignoring him.

"...And of course they want to sell it and rebuild."

"Ma'am?"

"I said the elders want sell the old church...the ruins...and rebuild, probably on Meeting Street if they can find a site."

Jason immediately grew interested. "How much would they ask for it?"

"Couldn't be much, it's burned crispy. This day and time I doubt they could get a hundred dollars."

"Really? The parsonage too?"

"Well, of course not the parsonage. Just the church. They don't have the money, or the inclination to tear it down and rebuild it when all they would have to do on Meeting Street is build the church."

"Only a hundred dollars?" That was what Sophia gave Dr. Gainey that day, that didn't sound like much.

"I'm not sure of the price. They want the buyer to promise to rebuild it for another congregation. Now that's ridiculous. Who has money to spend on building a church? Unless, of course, it's another church."

"Who is the minister here now?"

"There isn't one. You don't need a minister when you don't really have a church. The elders hold meetings in their homes. They've split up the congregation among themselves. And they aren't paying me. They let me live here if I take care of the place.

Her constant chatter faded from Jason's consciousness as a plan–an absurd plan–began to form in his mind. He would buy the church. He would rebuild it. He would turn it into a mission for his starving and dying people. He would preach the Word of God to their hearts, feed their bellies and provide shelter for their heads. He only needed one thing. Money. And someone to buy it for him. Nobody would sell a 19-year-old Negro a church, especially a white man's church.

Jason dashed home and had a long talk with Aunt Catherine.

"We could call it the Church of the Three Crosses. They would never ask you any questions."

"You want me to tell them I represent the Church of the Three Crosses and buy the Lambol Methodist for a hundred dollars?" Catherine was disbelieving. "Jason, I don't have a hundred dollars."

"I'll get it...from somewhere. I need you to buy it because I am a Negro. And you have to say it's a church that's buying it."

"You want me to lie to a church to buy a church?"

"It won't be a lie. It will be the Church of the Three Crosses."

"But a black church? On Lambol?"

"All colors will be welcome. No one will be turned away."

Catherine could see the bubbling enthusiasm.

Slowly she evolved from disbelieving to amused. It was a ridiculous idea, and, she decided, impossible. Nevertheless, she humored him.

"Alright, Jason. When you get the money, I'll represent you and buy Lambol Methodist for the Church of Three Crosses."

Jason was elated. Half the dream was accomplished. Now for the money.

CHAPTER 23

In spite of the fact that Fitz was one of only a handful of students in the history of the school who had been accelerated, he graduated at the top of his class. He was an extremely happy young man of nineteen. He was through his schooling; he was going home. He and Mary were to be married in three days. Monty's support of this union, though not necessary, was much appreciated by the young couple.

"After all," Monty had said, "she's a wonderful girl, and of course you Americans are free of this peerage-commoner complication.

The day before the wedding, Fitz dropped by Monty's bank. "I've booked passage for Mary and me for the day after the wedding, Monty. We'll honeymoon on the voyage home."

"Splendid. I'll be going with you. It's time I informed your father of his unbelievable gain in wealth, and of your amazing propensity for making money. My God, you've become a shipping magnate and you're barely nineteen.

"Monty, ah... why don't you come on the next ship. Your presence could prove a bit awkward. I mean, ah, the honeymoon and all."

"My God, that's true. How thoughtless of me. What ship are you taking?

"The Mary-Em. It's her maiden voyage."

"Oh, and what a beauty she is, the flagship of the Manigault shipping company. You are wise to buy only steam ships, Fitz. The clippers are good, but their days are numbered."

"Monty, It was a joint decision. Your advice swung it."

"Well, I do what I can," Monty feigned modesty.

"And the coal mine you purchased for us," Fitz continued. "That was a stroke of genius. Wood burning is so inefficient, and we will own our own fuel supply plus make a profit selling the coal."

"The Mary-Em, Fitz?" Mary asked that evening at dinner.

"Yes, the Mary-Em. I named her for you."

Mary smiled. "That was sweet of you."

"Well Manigault shipping will be half yours, Mary. We've only seventeen ships, but we will grow."

"Only seventeen?" Monty interjected. "Seventeen is not 'only', especially when they're all the finest, most modern ships plowing the seas."

"I want more. Europe needs cotton and tobacco. America needs everything. This is a good time for shipping."

"It's always a good time for shipping, my boy. You're going to be one of the worlds wealthiest men."

"I want to be, Monty. But not for me, for my country. It has to be rebuilt."

"From what I've heard about the war, there may not be that much money on earth."

With that Mary rose. The men came to their feet.

"I'll leave you to your talk," she said. "Tomorrow is the most important day of my life. I'm going to retire early."

"Good night, Mary," said Monty.

"Good night, my love," said Fitz.

Someone who did not know the situation might have thought that a Duke of the realm was getting married. The church was filled to capacity to see the young rich man from America marry a British commoner. There were mixed emotions. Some thought the informality of the Americans was wonderful. Others were aghast that such a union could take place. But when Mary came down the aisle, her radiant beauty glowing for all to see, they were unanimous. Fitz was a lucky man.

No one knew this more than Fitz himself as he watched her

approaching on the arm of her father. Monty, his best man, stood by his side. At that very moment, yet another Manigault steamer was leaving the shipyard at Liverpool for trial at sea.

Their cabin aboard the Mary-Em was magnificent. Especially decorated for them. It was the height of luxury and convenience.

"It's exquisite, Fitz," Mary exclaimed as he carried her through the door. "But I shall see only you."

"Perhaps for a while. But this is our home for the next few weeks. You'll see it."

There was a polite knock at the door. It was the captain.

"Welcome aboard, Mr. Manigault, Mrs. Manigault."

"Thank you, Captain." Fitz shook his hand.

"I trust everything is to your satisfaction?"

"Indeed it is, sir."

"There is one feature I thought I would bring to your attention, sir. This bell pull, yank it twice for assistance and a cabin boy will respond. Yank it three times if you wish your meal served here in you cabin, otherwise it is my pleasure to have you dine at the Captain's table."

"This is most thoughtful of you, Captain. We are most appreciative," Mary said. "I do believe I would prefer to have supper in the cabin tonight."

"Splendid. I'll inform the galley. Just yank the pull when you're ready."

He saluted and departed, leaving them alone.

Everything had been unpacked and put away for them.

"I think I'm going to enjoy being rich, Fitz," Mary said laughingly.

That first night in their cabin, Mary looked at him with dancing, mischievous eyes.

"Well now, this won't be much of a honeymoon for you, my bonnie lad. I've nothing new or different to offer."

"I'll just have some more of the same, and you may drop the Scottish accent."

She giggled. "Very well. Hand me my night gown."

"No gown, lady. It gets in the way!"

She giggled again as she fell back across the bed nude, opening her legs seductively.

"Don't wink at me, young lady, unless you want a finger in your eye." He fell upon her and kissed her passionately. "I love you, Mary."

"I love you, Fitz," she gasped. "Are you in a hurry?"

"I'm always in a hurry with you."

"Slow down. I want this to last an eternity."

He kissed her again as she began to moan and move with him. Then she rolled him over on his back.

"I'll take charge for awhile," she cooed. As she smiled down on him, moving rhythmically, her breasts swung freely like bells above his face. He played his tongue across her nipples. The sensation caused her to arch her back even more and brought a giggle from deep in her throat. Then, as their breathing grew heavier, they exploded together. She collapsed in his arms and for long minutes they lay quietly, regaining their strength, their composure.

The following morning, as they strolled on the deck arm in arm, Mary said: "Fitz, it is something of a shock. There must be a hundred passengers, yet I feel you and I are the only people for hundreds of miles."

"I like that feeling, darling. I hope you will always feel that way. I know I will."

Fitz and the Captain gave her a tour of the entire ship from the engine room to the bridge. "Pay attention, Mary," Fitz said. "Someday you may have to run this shipping company for me." She listened and watched intently and asked pointed, intelligent questions by the dozens. Fitz was proud of her. She had a keen, inquiring mind. Every fact she heard was catalogued and stored for later use.

It would have been impossible for two people to be more in love or more caring for each other. Often they spoke of business in serious, informing conversations.

"Fitz, the ship is lovely. But next time you'll be wanting a woman's touch when decorating the passenger's cabins. Now, we need..."

But more often, they played.

"Fitz! What are you doing? I'll give you twenty minutes to stop that!"

Day and night, the great ship steamed toward Charleston, toward the very dock where Jason had found work.

CHAPTER 24

Jason had been working with the longshoremen for a week by the time Fitz and Mary boarded the Mary-Em. When he was paid at the end of each day, he stared into his palm at the thirty-five cents and said his thanks to God. But thirty-five cents a day, he would have to work two hundred and eighty-six days for the hundred dollars for the burned out church. That was too long. Someone may beat him to it. He was constantly in turmoil hoping for another way to find the money.

They were unloading an English ship one afternoon when Jason overheard a conversation between the ship's Captain and a Charleston merchant.

"I can't wait two weeks, man! I must get under sail in four days! Now can you fill my order in that time or not?" he demanded of the merchant.

"Most of the silver and pewter is being horded by the black marketers. Their prices are exorbitant. I can't make a profit if I buy..."

"Blast it man. We had a deal! You promised me five tons and you're almost a ton short."

"I can fill the order in two weeks."

"And I will have sailed a week and a half before then! Good day to you sir!"

"I'll do what I can, but..." The captain walked away in a huff.

Suddenly Jason saw the solution to his problem. "Excuse me, Captain," Jason called out as he started toward him.

Before he ran ten feet a sailor stepped in his way and slapped him hard across the mouth with the back of his hand. Jason went reeling, tumbling backward. Blood was gushing from his lip, spattering the deck.

"Don't address the Cap'n, niggah," the sailor moved toward him threateningly.

"I can get him more cargo," Jason muttered.

"What did you say, niggah?"

"I can get him more cargo!" Jason shouted, infuriated.

"Get off the ship, niggah, before I run you through." He reached for his sword.

"Wait!" It was the Captain. He walked over to where Jason lay on the deck.

"How can you do that?" the Captain asked.

"We hid it from the Yankees."

That was all he needed to say. The countryside was ripe with rumors of great treasures being buried ahead of the Federal advance. The Captain had heard them too.

"What kind of cargo?" he asked Jason.

"Silver, pewter, paintings, silk, linen..."

"Where? Where is it?"

"The Manigault plantation."

"Bring him to my cabin," the captain ordered.

Just the two of them in the cabin soon came to an understanding. The Captain would furnish a wagon and four men. Jason would take them to the plantation. They would return with the treasure, the Captain would evaluate it and pay him a fair price.

It took most of two days to return with the Manigault's most precious possessions. It was dark when they placed the barrels in the hold and the Captain inspected them.

"Exquisite," was all he said. He nodded his head. Two men grabbed Jason and dragged him topside. He just had time to notice the ship was under sail before the two men heaved him over the side. They thought he would drown. Most blacks could not swim, but thanks to Fitz, Jason could.

As he sprawled on the pier trying to catch his breath, Jason was at the lowest point on his life. He had betrayed a sacred trust, stolen from those who had given him everything. Yes, he had told himself it was wrong, but it was a wrong that would ultimately do much good for his people. Jason would never forget again. Nothing good can come from anything dishonest, anything evil.

He walked back to Catherine's carriage house with heavy steps. Everyone was asleep when he arrived. He had not been home for two days. No one had seemed to notice. He spent a sleepless night listening to the old ones snore, a young one with an occasional nightmare, trying to decide how God would punish him. He loved his Bible dearly. He loved every word it said, every adventure it described. But was it God he loved...or was it the power of knowledge? He was not sure. Only his mother and father, beside himself, knew of the buried valuables. Mr. Mitchell was dead and Sophia was missing. Perhaps it would never be missed. But would not living a lie make things worse?

The next morning was Sunday. He taught the children Sunday School and read Matthew to the old ones. Then he went into the yard and sat in the sun.

"Jason?" It was Catherine. "You look terribly sad this morning."

"Yes, Ma'am."

"Well, I suspect that won't last long because I have wonderful news for you! Fitz is coming home!"

Jason jumped up grinning from ear to ear. "That's wonderful."

Then he thought of his theft again. How could he face Fitz?

"Yes," Catherine continued. "They should land Thursday. You and I will met them. Oh, we are saved! Fitz will fix everything! You'll see! She returned to the house.

Jason walked to Lambol and stood in front of the burned-out church. He looked up at the blackened cross, leaning precariously, silhouetted against a brilliant blue Charleston sky.

"Dear Lord. If it be thy will, here I will begin my ministry. Here I will teach, and feed, and care for my people who are starving and afraid, ignorant and hopeless. From this point I will spread your Word across the land like a rolling tide that will engulf the black man in good works and in service to you. But I cannot do it alone. I need your help, dear Lord. I need your miracles. Just plainly spoken, Lord, I need a hundred dollars. Oh, I know a hundred dollars will only buy the ruins. It will take thousands to rebuild. It will take thousands upon tens of thousands to reach my goal. But can't we just start with the hundred, Lord? I have ten. Maybe you could scare up ninety?"

At that very moment the cross atop the church gave way. It came crashing to the ground, splintering in a cloud of soot and dust.

"If that is a sign, Lord, I don't know what it means, but I'm going to take it to mean you're helping me get the damage out of the way so we can rebuild."

It would take him awhile to believe that, so he turned and walked back to Catherine's.

CHAPTER 25

At ten o'clock Thursday morning, Catherine and Jason stood on the dock watching the approach of the Mary-Em. She was right on schedule. A two-mile long ribbon of smoke danced from her stacks to the horizon in the calm morning air. Within an hour she was tied up and her gangplank being lowered. Fitz and Mary were the first passengers off the ship. After hugging Catherine and introducing Mary, Fitz turned to his old playmate.

"Jason," he said simply, tears in his eyes.

Jason extended his hand. Ignoring it, Fitz threw his arms around him.

"My God, it's good to see you!"

"It's good to see you too, Master Fitz." He felt so awkward.

"To hell with that Jason. It's me; it's Fitz. I haven't changed."

With that Jason burst into tears and let himself go. He threw his arms around Fitz and the two of them laughed and cried and pounded each other on the back.

"Mary, this is Jason."

"Hello, Jason," she smiled broadly and extended her hand. "I feel as though I've known you forever."

Jason was not what she expected. He was gaunt, dressed in little better than rags. She had expected a man, bigger than life, who glowed with intelligence. That is how Fitz's descriptions had made him seem.

He took her hand. She was even more beautiful than he imagined.

"Have you heard from Mama and Papa, Catherine?" I had hoped they could meet us."

"I'll catch you up when we get home, Fitz. Now let's be on our way."

That night Jason lay on his bed of straw with emotions running rampant. Somehow, in his heart, he wanted them to invite him inside, with the family. But he was with his family out here in the carriage house. Little things kept happening to remind him that he was not quite a man–in the eyes of white people. Fitz loved him, yes. He knew that. But still there was a barrier between them. It was this barrier that prevented him from being in the house exchanging views. But no, he was black. His place was in the stable. He vowed it would not always be that way. He would rise to be equal to the white man. And he would raise as many of his brethren with him as he possibly could.

Had Jason known of the grief inside the house, and inside Fitz, he would not have been so anxious to be there.

When the first rays of the sun flashed across Charleston, Jason was up and starting for work. Across the yard he saw Fitz sitting on the porch staring into the brightening sky.

"Fitz?"

Fitz looked up. "Mornin' Jason."

"Fitz, I'm sorry. There was nothing we could do."

"You did your best, old friend. Thank you for that."

"I will always wish I could have done more."

"Where are you going?"

"To work."

"Where?"

"On the docks. I help load and unload the ships."

"Have you had breakfast?"

"We only eat once a day, Fitz. Mrs. Catherine can't do better."

"We'll change that, Jason. Today! You all need clothes, too."

We really don't want to stay here and eat Catherine out of everything she has, Fitz. You can't believe how hard it is to find work. And the whites on the docks make ten times more than the Negroes who get only thirty-five cents a day!" Jason sat down.

"What? That's ridiculous."

"It's life here in Charleston."

"Well, you don't go to work today, Jason. I'm hiring you for fifteen dollars a day.

"Doing what?"

"I haven't decided."

Fitz looked toward the rising sun and sighed again.

"Why don't we walk awhile, Fitz?"

"Good idea."

The two old friends rose and went down the sidewalk together. They were almost the same size and build. Their gait's were even similar.

"I missed you, Fitz."

"And I you, Jason."

"Wouldn't it be great if we could go back to those times."

"I'd give my arm," Fitz said. "However, I notice I wouldn't have to correct your English anymore."

"I thank you for the compliment. Actually, I speak two languages. White and nigger. I have to be careful to speak the right one at the right time."

"I wish you wouldn't say 'nigger'. Mama hated that word.

"I've earned the right to say it, Fitz."

"That sounds something like one of the bricks in the wall I feel going up between us, Jason."

"It is. And yes, I feel it too. I hope we can tear it down instead of making it bigger."

"We don't have to tear it down, Jason. Let's just not ever build it."

"Are you going back to the Manigault, Fitz?"

"I doubt it. The Manigault doesn't exist anymore. Oh, I know the land is still there. And what's left of the house. But not the Manigaults. You see, Jason, the Manigault was not the land and buildings. It was the people. It was my parents' decency. Their dreams. Their love for each other and for you and your people. That's all gone now. I doubt we will, or even can, go back."

"What will you do?"

"I have plans. The question is: what will you do, Jason?"

"I'll show you. Come with me. It isn't far. I've done a lot of growing up since you left. And I have learned a lot of things. Things, perhaps, you don't know."

"Like what?"

"For one thing, life on the Manigault was a far cry from the lives most of my people had. I've heard them talking. Children torn from their mothers and sold for profit, men and women beaten to death or shot. Women being bred like cattle to produce babies for the slave market. Awful, ungodly things, Fitz. Things that totally destroyed the dignity of so many of my people."

"I have heard of those things, Jason. But I never saw the cruelty first hand. How could Godly people act that way?"

"The point is—my people need help. More help than I can imagine. We have a whole race of people who not only need to be fed, housed, and educated, they need their dignity as men and women restored. It is an immense job that only God will be able to accomplish."

They continued to walk until they arrived at the church. Jason stopped and held up his arms.

"Here's my future, Fitz. Hopefully my destiny."

"It's a burned-out church."

"You see a burned church, I see a magnificent Cathedral filled with people. I see a place to feed the poor and care for the sick. I see a sanctuary for the homeless. I see a school for the ignorant, a training ground that will help them help themselves, white or black. I see God, in his infinite mercy, doing his work."

Fitz stared for a long while. "I think I can see it too, Jason. I also see you as the leader."

"God willing."

"Where are you going to get the money, Jason? I'm sorry. I think like a businessman now."

"I can buy the hull for one hundred dollars. Somehow I'll get it. I don't know how much the rest will be. But God will provide it."

"It's a beautiful dream, Jason. I'm sure he will provide."

It was midmorning when they returned to the house. Catherine and Mary were about to leave.

"Fitz," said Mary. "Catherine is taking me into town. We're going to refurnish the house and get a proper food supply. Do try to busy yourself. Good morning Jason."

"Good morning," Jason smiled back.

"Do you have any American money, Mary?" Fitz asked.

"Yes," Mary said. "But you had better visit the bank and make sure everything is in order with the Bank of England."

"Listen to her," Fitz winked at Jason. "She has taken over my business already."

CHAPTER 26

Within a month carpenters had turned the carriage house into comfortable quarters. Catherine's house was refilled with furnishings, and Meta and her helpers were preparing three meals a day. Abraham was happy that he, once more, had a beautiful home to run. Everyone was clothed properly and all of the blacks had been examined by a doctor.

"Jason," Fitz called. Bring the horses."

They were next door. Fitz had purchased the adjoining property to stable his horses.

"We're going for a ride. Bring one for yourself, too."

They rode side by side. Fitz led them down Lambol and Jason's heart sank. Workmen were cleaning the debris from the church.

"Oh, dear God!" Jason cried out loud. "Someone bought the church."

"Yes," Fitz said. "It would appear that way."

They reined up. In a moment a small man emerged from the building carrying a roll of paper. He saw the two horsemen and walked toward them.

"Good morning, Mr. Manigault."

"Good morning, Archibald," Fitz called out.

"And might this be Reverend Apelligo?"

"Yes," Fitz said. "Jason, this is Archibald Bradly. He is your architect. I'm sure you two have much to discuss."

"What! I...? What? I'm not a reverend..."

"This is your church, Jason. Tell him how you want it rebuilt." Fitz rode away, "I'll see you at suppertime."

"But...I...Fitz! What have you done?"

Fitz laughed and continued up Lambol Street.

"But you can't just ride away, Fitz!" Jason yelled.

"I have to. I'm meeting Monty at the docks. He's due at noon."

"I feel, Reverend Apelligo, that we should get the feel of the property before I begin drawing. You'll have a better idea of what you want."

"How much money are we talking abut spending, Mr. Bradley?"

"Mr. Manigault has no set figure in mind."

"I see. Very well, I can tell you now, Mr. Bradley, I want the sanctuary just the way it was. As for the rest, let's start looking. But please, let's try to keep the cost down.

"Mr. Manigault also purchased the parsonage. You may need to know that."

"I see. Yes I do. And the lady who lives there, what about her?"

"She'll be moving out, I'm sure."

"Excuse me for a moment, Mr. Bradley."

Jason went over to the parsonage and knocked. Mrs. Manly answered.

"Hello, Jason. How are you, my boy?"

Jason ignored the question. "Mrs. Manly, I wanted to tell you that you don't have to move."

"Really?" She smiled. "But the house has been sold, dear boy."

"It was bought by a friend of mine. He wishes to keep the same agreement you had with the elders for the time being."

"Oh, thank God! I didn't know where I could go."

"If you ever leave this house, Mrs. Manly, it will be your choice. I promise you that."

She looked puzzled, but said, "Thank you, Jason. Are you sure?"

"I am sure. I'll see you again soon. Good day, Mrs. Manly."

"Good day, Jason. And God bless you."

"He has, dear lady, he has."

Monty and Fitz went to work immediately establishing the new head office of Manigault Shipping in Charleston along with its complex financial arms that reached out in every direction. Manigault ships were sailing on every sea of the world, faster than almost every competitor and with better rates and more efficiency. New Manigault ships steamed out of Liverpool as quickly as they could be built. But still the cash reserves continued building to astronomical levels.

"Fitz, we really need to find new areas to invest. You are cash heavy." Monty dropped his pen and rubbed his eyes.

"I know. We could give it away."

"You've already given eight hundred thousand dollars to your charities. You're going to have to give it away faster than that or create new investments."

"My heart is here in South Carolina. I'd prefer to invest it here."

"There is little here but agriculture, Fitz. That limits things."

"We can start some manufacturing. How about an iron works?"

"Iron? We would have to ship in the ore, the coal...I don't know, the shipping costs would make it difficult to turn a profit, I should think."

Fitz brightened. "Not if we owned the railroad."

"But the railroads are in a shambles. The North all but destroyed them forever."

"Exactly! We should be able to get a good buy. Then we could rebuild ourselves."

"Of course." Monty began thinking fast. "There's bound to be Federal money to help rebuild. It might be touch and go for a while, but potential profits, just from the railroad...Fitz, lets forget the ironworks for the moment. Let's get into railroading. We can tie Manigault shipping from all over the world into interior distribution. We can tie the South together and ship its products everywhere. Profits all over the place!"

"Monty, sometimes I think profit is all you ever think about. I want to help rebuild the South."

"So do I, Fitz. But we have to have substantial profit to do it."
"Then it's settled. We buy a railroad."
"Agreed," said Monty. "Maybe several." His mind was racing.

Monty's international business connections established over his years of banking, plus the combination of his and Fitz's finances made them an awesome power. Practically everyone in the South was destitute. There weren't a hundred men left to take fair advantage of the opportunities presented by a nation on its knees. Fitz and Monty could literally overwhelm any competition from the Yankees. They needed to go full steam ahead because both of them suspected the North, in its punitive disposition, would attempt to rape anything and everything of value still remaining.

Within six months, they owned the Manigault-Hastings Railroad. North Carolina, Georgia, Tennessee and all of South Carolina would soon terminate at Charleston Harbor and then radiate across the seven seas.

CHAPTER 27

"Mrs. Manly, I wonder if I could have a few minutes of your time?"
Jason stood on the parsonage steps.

"Come in, Jason. I've seen you at the church every day for weeks. Are you working with the builders?"

"In a manner of speaking, Mrs. Manly."

"Won't you sit down?"

"Thank you." Jason sat on the edge of the chair. "Mrs. Manly, the truth of the matter is, the church is being rebuilt by Fitzsimmons Manigault. He also bought the parsonage."

"Well now, isn't that nice. But they're already building the new church on Meeting Street."

"Oh, he's not rebuilding it for them, Mrs. Manly. He's building it for me."

"For you, Jason?" she laughed. Then she realized he was serious. "Oh, I didn't...I'm sorry.

In spite of himself Jason felt his anger rise. Even though she had said nothing degrading, the air was ripe with her prejudices.

"Yes, for me. I'm going to make it a school, a refuge for the poor, and a church." He found himself speaking more strongly than he wanted.

"I'm sorry, Jason. I meant no offense. It's just that..."

"That I'm a nigger."

"You know I don't mean that." She appeared hurt. "But honestly, yes. Old feelings die hard. I'm no bigot, but..." her voice dropped to a whisper, "Old feelings die hard."

Jason's hurt did not subside.

"I came here to offer you a position as my housekeeper, Mrs. Manly."

She was totally shocked for a moment, so much so that she gasped.

"I...well, I don't know...I..."

"I understand," said Jason.

"Wait, it's so fast...so surprising."

"Don't you mean bazaar? A white woman keeping house for a Negro?"

"Well, yes. I suppose."

"Why don't I give you a chance to think about it?" And to himself he said, "And me time to cool off."

"That would be nice."

Jason said his goodbyes and left.

He thought about the conversation. As he did, he became more and more angry. He had offered this woman a job, a home. He had expected her to jump at such an opportunity. But she was hesitant. Amused. Shocked.

"Mama," he said to his mother that evening. "Why would she react like that?"

"Boy, don't you know that if she keeps house for you, she'll be the talk of Charleston? She won't have one friend left. People will call he a niggah lover and will think all kinds of terrible things about her...and you.

"You keep house for Catherine and the Manigaults and nobody says nothin'."

"Boy, you got to know better than that. A Negro working for a white is the natural order of things. A white working for a Negro... especially a white woman for a Negro man...that just ain't natural."

"Well times are changing."

"You sure you don't want to do this for some bad reason? To make a point about somethin'? You can get plenty of Negro housekeepers."

"I'm being nice to her. I'm offering to let her keep her job and her home."

"Are you really sure 'bout that."

"It started out that way. She was good to me when I was with Dr. Gainey. I thought I was a person to her."

"But Dr. Gainey was there. Nobody thought she was going to your bed in the middle of the night. They would think that now."

"Would you think that, Mama?"

"White men like Negro women, Jason. I reckon it works both ways."

"You know that for a fact, Mama?" Jason's eyes narrowed.

"You ain't too big for a whippin' yet, boy. And I'll tell you something else. You ain't half so damn smart as you thinks you is. I ain't never seen no nigger wants to be white so bad as you."

Jason had never seen his mother so angry. She slammed the door behind her. *What is going on here? I'm getting everything-the church, a chance to have my own congregation, everything I've wanted and people are rejecting me. By God, I am going to lead people and they, his critics, can all go to hell. Including Mama.*

When he reached the church the following morning, the workers were already there. He looked toward the parsonage with a strong sense of dread...and anger. He put off going to see Mrs. Manly until late afternoon. It was a very sober-faced Mrs. Manly who answered the door.

"Come in, Jason." This time she served tea.

Jason remained silent except the "thank you" when she handed him his cup and saucer.

"Jason, I'm not sure you understand what a tremendous decision this is for me."

"Perhaps not." Jason's anger rose again. "But I think I have some idea."

"If I take the job, I will be ostracized from my friends and family."

"Perhaps so. "So if you wish to refuse..."

"Please, Jason. Hear me out."

"I'm sorry, please continue."

"I can live with that under certain conditions."

Jason looked up at her. "Go on."

"How many people will live here?"

"Just you and me, Mrs. Manly."

"I have your word on that? You won't bring in a staff?"

"You mean, will I bring a dozen niggers in here to live?"

"I meant a staff of teachers or administrators or whatever."

"No. Just me."

"Then I have your word on that?"

"You do."

"If I do this, I must make more of a contribution than just cleaning. Will you allow me to teach at the school?"

"Are you a qualified teacher?"

"When I was married, I taught school in Savannah for two years. When my husband died, I moved to Charleston and have been here ever since."

"You will be my first teacher."

Mrs. Manly sighed heavily. She walked to the window and studied the workmen as they placed the third cross. The three crosses stood regally against a reddening sky as the sun began to set. They literally glowed. The beauty of it was sufficient to help with her decision.

"Very well, Jason. I will stay. And I thank you for your kindness."

Jason felt that he should have been happy about her decision, but he wasn't. The entire episode had been traumatic for him. At that moment, he didn't know why.

"Fine," he said. He forced a smile.

"Will you be moving in soon?"

"In a few days when the church and educational wing are finished. The hospital wing has a way to go yet."

"I'll prepare Dr. Gainey's room and his study for you."

Jason rose to leave.

"One more thing, Jason."

"Yes."

"Will you...I'm not sure how to ask it. Will you...be expecting sexual favors?"

"What?"

She reddened.

"Did old Dr. Gainey?"

"Yes, I'm afraid so."

Jason was at a loss for words. Finally he said, "I think not, Mrs. Manly. You see, I am already married...to my faith."

She stood quietly, eyes averted.

Again Jason started for the door. Upon reaching it, he could not help himself. He turned and asked: "Mrs. Manly, when you made you decision to stay, did you think that a possibility?"

After a long moment of silence, her eyes met his and she said simply, "Yes."

He left. It was on his way home that he realized he had always thought of Mrs. Manly as a little old spinster lady. Now he knew she was an educated widow. He judged her as being in her late thirties or early forties. In spite of himself, it was exciting to know she had, among her decision making thoughts, accepted the idea of sleeping with him. But he fought that feeling, recalling what Meta had said. Besides, he had never been with any woman. He wouldn't know what to do anyway. And fornication was a sin. He was already a thief, having stolen the Manigault buried treasure. Worse yet, he had betrayed Fitz in the process. Now he was forced to live a lie, to accept his friend's unbounded generosity, to feel more and more like the thief he was. He swore he would not include fornication to further blacken his already terribly flawed soul. He so envied Fitz. Fitz and Mary were unbelievably happy and in love. Fitz was in command everywhere he went. The biggest, most important men around treated him with respect. They all feared his power and his intellect.

"I want to be powerful, too," he thought. "But not through money, no. Through love and respect for what I do for my people." But he knew without Fitz's money, his unending generosity, he would never realize his dream. Fitz was a tool of God's. Jason hoped to be.

That evening Abraham called Jason from the carriage house. "Mista Fitz wants to see you. He's in the study."

"Yes, Papa."

When Jason entered, Fitz was working on rows of figures. He looked up and laid down his pen.

"Sit down, Jason. The church is finished. So is the educational building. I guess you need to go to work. Your salary is increased to one hundred dollars a week."

"Fitz...I'm still not sure what this is all about."

"I guess I have been too busy, Jason. When you told me about what you wanted, you know, the church, the school, the meals for the poor...well, I agreed with you. It was, and is, a great idea. The facility is yours. No strings attached. But I'm not going to leave you hanging either. What you have in mind will not generate any income for a long, long time. And you need operating funds. You'll need cooks, teachers, at least one doctor, nurses..."

I hadn't thought too much about that yet."

"No but you need to. Right away. Do you have any idea how many pupils you will have?" How many teachers you'll need? How many people you'll feed? Care for medically?"

"Well, no. I haven't."

"You're a dreamer, Jason. I know we need dreamers. You can thank God that I'm a practical man. I have the figures. I've projected your expenses based upon the facility's capacity and an assumption of zero income. The Church of the Three Crosses has a bank balance, as of yesterday morning, of one hundred thousand dollars."

The figure boggled Jason's mind.

"That's your start-up money and your first year's budget combined. I've appointed Sellers and Sellers as your accounting firm. They will handle all financial transactions for you. If at any time, you need..."

They talked far into the night. Actually, Fitz talked. Jason listened. He received a liberal education in finance that evening. Early the following morning, he arose and began his quest for the right people to staff the Church of the Three Crosses.

For the next few months, Fitz and Monty were on the road most of the time seeing to the repairs of the hundreds of miles of track, to the purchase of cars and engines, and to hiring the best railroad people they could find. As always they paid top wages and bought the finest quality. It would not be long until the railroads ran themselves through the highly efficient and qualified cadre they hired.

Fitz and Monty were not unnoticed by politicians and businessmen alike. With Fitz's wealth and business acumen, he was easily the most powerful man in South Carolina, if not in the entire South.

Soon the military government dissolved and turned South Carolina over to the carpetbaggers and scallywags. They all yearned, in some way, to take the Manigault fortune for themselves.

CHAPTER 28

As Fitz came through the office door, Monty said, "Fitz, have you seen the tax notice for the railroad?"

"No."

"It's twenty-two million dollars!"

"What? That's the value of the whole damn thing."

"I know."

"They want it badly, don't they?"

"You know, your plantation is even worse by comparison."

'How do you mean?"

"The scallywags are buying land for ten cents an acre...that's the going rate. Your taxes on the Manigault are two hundred thousand dollars. That's about a thousand times its worth."

"Monty, we're going to Columbia. We're going to visit the governor."

Fitz and Monty had no problem scheduling a meeting.

"I had hoped," said Fitz to the governor, "that this meeting would never be necessary."

He handed him the tax notices for the railroad and the Manigault.

"Mr. Manigault," the governor said as he studied the documents, "surely you understand that reconstructing the South will require vast resources. Everyone must pay his share. After all, you are one of the wealthiest men in the country."

"You need not continue, sir," said Fitz. "I have no intention of draining my resources to line the pockets of this collection of thieves and hoodlums you have the audacity to call a government."

The governor's face hardened as the smile faded. "I beg your pardon."

"Come off it man! We're adult people here. These are not taxes. This is out and out undisguised thievery! You know it! Kindly do not insult my intelligence."

"I believe, Mr. Manigault, this meeting is at an end. The government will simply have to foreclose."

"If you value your position, Governor, this meeting is not even close to ending. You had better listen very carefully."

Something in Fitz's voice and eyes seem to make the governor sit back in his chair and say: "Very well, sir. I will listen."

"First," Fitz rose and began pacing, "if you persist in this and foreclose, I will guarantee you not one hundred yards of usable track, not one working engine, not one available railroad man will be left.

Then Fitz placed his hands on the governor's desk and leaned across it. "And Manigault Shipping will avoid South Carolina's ports and every shipping company in the entire world will follow suit. This state will dry up like a leaf in winter. Oh, you'll wind up owning all the land, but you won't be able to give it away!"

Silence. Fitz straightened up and returned to his chair.

The governor thought for a moment. "What do you propose, Mr. Manigault?"

"Fair taxes and no interference from your so called 'government'," he spat the word.

What do you consider fair?"

"Fair would be to not levy taxes and allow me to plow hat money back into the state with jobs and services. However, I'm willing to pay eighty mills of a fair appraisal."

The governor thought again. "I'll see what I can do, Mr. Manigault. But I can't make any promises."

"You still don't understand, Governor. I have the resources to move my operation anywhere in the world. Too much harassment from your government and I damn well will. But I promise you this.

Before I do, I'll punish this state for the inconvenience. So you damn well better get it done!"

The governor was beaten. He knew it. With the state being in the situation it was, economically, pickings were slim. Manigault could ruin the whole party. Fitz knew it and would not even allow him a token saving of face.

"I'll expect my new tax notices next week. Kindly don't disappoint me. And by the way, the same goes for everything I own. Let's go, Monty."

They left without a goodbye.

"You can be ruthless, Fitz," Monty said as they reached the Capitol steps.

"The idea of that white trash and his thieves trying to push us around..."

Monty smiled. Fitz had learned his craft well.

The new tax notices came. Fitz was spared the outright larceny to which most of the state was subjected. His purpose was not his own personal gain. He wanted to help the people of his state. To do that, he had to keep his holdings intact. He hired a team of men who went around the countryside buying land at public auctions and returning the deeds to the rightful owners. It was a stopgap measure, and expensive. Fitz hoped things would change soon, but had no illusions about it.

Meanwhile, the Church of the Three Crosses was in full operation. Mrs. Manly had thirty-one students ranging in ages from five to fourteen. She started them all from the same point, the ABCs. The kitchen was feeding two hundred to three hundred meals a day. The hospital wing, designed for thirty beds, had forty-three patients. Mostly they were old, undernourished. The church cemetery had a fresh grave almost daily. On Sundays, Jason held services. They were simple and straightforward. Jason decided he would only preach on God's love and on hope for the future. He could not bring himself to preach condemnation to these poor people. They had gone through so much! It was as if a whole generation of people were doomed to live in a state of shock and helplessness. He wanted to lessen the pain, not instill fear.

The reputation of the Church of the Three Crosses spread like wildfire across the south People came from everywhere. Soon Jason added to his staff. Two men...yes, they were white...to find jobs and homes for the Negroes. There were whites as well as blacks in the hospital, the cafeteria, and the congregation. Jason turned no one away who was in need. But there were no whites in the school. Schools for Negroes were too scarce to forfeit one precious desk. There were many schools for whites.

Occasionally, Fitz would go over Jason's books at Sellers and Sellers. Not to check on him, but to offer advice.

"It always impresses me, Jason. You do so much with so little. But I think you are cutting too many corners."

"I try to be careful with your money, Fitz."

"I see you are feeding people for four cents a meal. Are they getting any meat?"

"Some."

"I recommend you double your food budget, Jason."

"If I do, I'd rather double the number of people we're feeding. The food is filling, and healthy enough."

"Then quadruple it. You're holding the spending too tight."

Jason heaved a sigh. He was not happy with Fitz's criticism, but he simply said: "It's your money Fitz."

"Damn it, Jason. It's not my money. It's God's money. It's simply being funneled through me to you."

That hurt. Fitz's business, his life-style, his demeanor did not appear to be blatantly Christian. Yet, he had just reminded Jason of a basic premise of every good Christian. All good things come from God–all good things are God's. Sure, the devil has money, and lots of it. But it is not used for good.

Fitz sensed Jason's mood swing.

"I'm sorry. I'm not trying to tell you how to do your work. You have dedicated your whole life to this. I suppose I'm just trying to tell you not to think of it as my money and hold back. I expect and hope that your financial outlay will grow, not diminish."

Jason did not appear to be appeased, so he continued. "I only give the Church of the Three Crosses a fraction of what I give to other charities. I'm making money so fast I can't get it reinvested, so you're doing me a favor. Hell's bell's man, every dime I give away, my profits seem to increase two fold."

Jason brightened. "That's the way of the Lord. Cast your bread upon the waters..."

"Exactly, old friend. By the way, I've purchased the adjoining property on both sides of the church. I think you and Archibald should put your heads together on what you need to do with it."

"My God, Fitz. That gives the whole block!"

"That was my goal from the beginning."

"It must have cost you a fortune."

"There you go again. No," he said hesitantly. "Quite frankly, Jason, with all the activity you have here, the owners were only too glad to sell."

"Oh, I'm sorry."

"It can't be helped. Prejudices run deep. It will take a hundred years...maybe a thousand... for that to change. Speaking of prejudice, how is Mrs. Manly adjusting to keeping house for a Negro?"

"I don't see much of her. She stays pretty much to her end of the house. I know she's been ostracized by her friends and family. But she's doing a great job with her classes."

"Good. She'll be all right. You'll see."

"I hope so. She's a fine lady."

"What are you paying her?"

"Room and board and five dollars a week."

"What?...Sorry, none of my business."

"I've been thinking of doubling it," Jason said with a grin.

They both laughed.

After Fitz left, Jason walked over to the church for his meeting. With him were the four brightest ministers he had been able to search out in the entire country. The brightest of the four was the Reverend Matthew Franklin, the head of the little task force Jason had assembled.

"Jason, we are receiving excellent response from the new

churches we have contacted. And, our efforts at organizing the churches we've been working with are also succeeding. The way things are going, I feel it will be necessary, rather soon, to form a Diocese."

"I have thought of that," Jason said. The churches, especially the newly forming ones, are terribly fragile. They all need each other's support. Especially, they all need our support and prayers."

"The Diocese will be necessary in seeing to their needs, shoring them up when necessary."

"In order to form it properly, we will need something akin to a convention where we can organize it and elect the leadership on a democratic basis," said one of the members.

"Yes. Even the people who draw up the guiding laws should be elected that way," stated another member.

"Perhaps we should ask every church to submit a proposal..."

"No, no. They don't have the expertise."

Jason sat quietly for an hour and listened. Finally, when it appeared they had all finished he said: "Gentlemen, I am impressed with the work you have done. I'm impressed with the thought and imagination you have put forward. Very frankly, when I decided the time had come for us to create a network of churches throughout the South to make an organized effort to help our people, I had no idea that men as capable as you existed. Thank you. You have worked tirelessly and selflessly for our goals. I have very little to offer. Please, go on with the plan and let us organize a Diocese to administer and support the Negro churches. Left alone, they will flounder and many could fail. But properly organized, I feel in my heart, they will prosper and so will our people. Don't worry about the finances, the Church of the three Crosses will see to your needs."

The meeting ended and the men went back to their work.

CHAPTER 29

"Fitz, It's hard to believe I've been here for two years. I simply have to go home and see to my affairs," Monty said.

"I've been dreading this day, Monty. You've been the most valuable person in the entire organization from the very first day."

"I know better than that, but I won't start that argument again."

"Monty, would you consider a proposal?"

"Like what?"

"We've gotten too big and ungainly to continue running everything from Charleston. I've been thinking of splitting the operation management wise. The Americas and the far east from Charleston, Europe and the near east from London."

"Makes sense."

"Here, we'll call it Manigault-Hastings. In London it will be Hastings-Manigault."

"I'd have to sell my interest in the bank," Monty mused aloud. "Frankly, I've already given the same thing a lot of thought. The moment I get home, I'll get started."

"Why don't you take a month off first?"

"How about two weeks?"

"Done."

"By the way, Fitz. How is the search for Sophia going?"

"Pinkerton has every available man on it. Only time will tell, I'm afraid. But even if she's dead, I need to know."

"I understand. On a happier note, the railroad is fully operational and at ninety percent capacity. We should reach one hundred percent within sixty days."

"Sorry, Monty. I don't have the heart to talk business after thinking of Mother. I'm going for a walk. We'll get into the railroad in the morning. Oh, when will you be leaving?"

"No firm plans yet. Within the month, I suppose."

"It will be a sad day for Mary and me."

"For me as well."

Fitz left the office and walked with no particular route or destination in mind. He walked past warehouse after warehouse of the Manigault Lines. Goods were going in and out at a constant rate. Work gang hurried back and forth in seeming confusion, though he knew there was very little wasted motion. Everyone spoke to him, from the warehouse managers and the foremen to the most menial water carrier. They all knew him. He knew almost everyone of them. Fitz was not an ivory tower manager. Twice, while walking among them, he stopped to help heave a heavy crate. Then he dusted his hands and continued his walk.

"Where did all this come from–and so fast?" he thought. "And will it go just as quickly? Or will it last a thousand years? Is there a day coming when the government will take it, gobble it up with taxes and tariffs? Will it matter? There's enough money here, in Britain, and particularly in Switzerland to support my family for a dozen generations."

His one ache, his one pain was Sophia. Yes, he grieved for his father. Yes, he had not the courage to return to the Manigault, to the land, to the house. But where was his mother? If he could find her, would he have the courage to take her home to the Manigault? He would rebuild it to a splendor one could only imagine...but only for her.

He found himself on Lambol Street, passing The Church of the Three Crosses. He stopped and watched. Dozens of children were playing in the yard. Several old people sat in the sun while crisply clad nurses wandered among them, seeing to their needs. They were not digging in the cemetery so often now. The program must have saved countless lives by this time. Poor Jason, he thought, he's a saint and he doesn't even think he's a good man. He thought about Pinkerton's initial report about Jason attempt to sell the Manigault silver and paintings. Poor Jason. He was trying to do the right thing–help people. But he can't know that I have forgiven him unless I let him know. He sighed heavily, then said aloud: "That would be too embarrassing. But Jason my friend, you are forgiven. You were never condemned. But that captain was. He will never command another ship in this lifetime. Manigault lines had seen to that." Fitz didn't like keeping a secret from Jason. But for the moment, he thought it best.

Then he saw Mary. She was sitting on the lawn reading to several old blacks who were listening with their eyes closed, or they were asleep. He walked over. Just as he arrived, she closed the book. The blacks had not been asleep. They all began thanking "Missy" for her reading.

"I see Jason has put to work," he said to Mary.

"He's infectious, Fitz. I thought I could help in some small way."

"Well, better out here reading than peeling potatoes in the kitchen."

"Ha! Funny you should mention that. That's how I spent the morning."

Archibald Bradley and Jason came around the corner of the building in animated conversation.

"Ah, Mr. Manigault," Archibald called. "You're just in time."

"Hello, Archibald, Jason," Fitz called out.

"Reverend Apelligo has developed a brilliant plan."

"What is that?"

"Reverend?" Archibald turned to Jason.

"Fitz, I've decided to build a trade school to teach my people a trade."

"I like that."

"Yes," said Archibald. "There's more to life than lifting and plowing."

Jason tolerated, politely, the interruption. "Mr. Bradley has designed a building for us that will accommodate two hundred students in carpentry, blacksmithing...we'll start with about eight different trades."

"It's a great idea! Manigault Shipping will always need trained men."

"It will be expensive," Archibald interjected again.

"Expense is a relative thing," Fitz said. "Human beings are extraordinarily valuable. Get on with it, Archibald. Sellars and Sellars will see to your needs."

The he turned to Mary. "Walk you home?"

"Thank you, Darling."

CHAPTER 30

Fitz looked around the room. The most influential men of South Carolina's low country were there. Momentarily, Fitz felt naked without Mary's presence. "Like no one is watching my back," he thought. He had no idea what the meeting was about. It was all rather mysterious. A messenger had come to his office with a letter that said: The Honorable Judge Lambeau requests your presence at his home tonight. Eight o'clock. Your presence is deemed essential. Please tell no one of this.

Had Fitz been with his father years before he would have remembered some of the faces from that meeting on secession. Most of the men were pleasant enough. Only Judge Lambeau and two of the other older men were hard-faced. But then, they had called the meeting.

"Gentlemen, if we might begin." The judge rapped his gavel on his desk. "We have called this meeting to discuss a problem more devastating than the Yankee invasion. I will turn the meeting over to Matthew Johnson to bring you up to date. Matthew?"

"Thank you, Judge, ah, Mr. Chairman."

"Mr. Chairman?" Fitz thought. "I must have missed the election."

"As we all know, the blood suckers in Columbia, our most esteemed legislature of scallywags and carpetbaggers, the carefully collected trash of an entire nation, are bleeding us white.

There was scattered laughter at the pun.

"Our streets are not safe for our women and children. Our property is being stolen daily through exorbitant taxes and unconstitutional laws that Washington does not even question. Gentlemen, we, the landowners and taxpayers of this great state, are unrepresented, and even victimized, at every level of government. It is only a matter of time before our demise, and the arrival of total chaos."

The room was silent. The truth of his words had absorbed every one of them. Only Fitz had stood up to the government and met threat with counter threat. But then, only Manigault Shipping was big and powerful enough to threaten a government.

Matthew Johnson continued, "In Tennessee, an organization has been formed. They call it the Ku Klux Klan. Unfortunate name admittedly." Another titter of laughter ran through the group. But it was not something funny that made them laugh, it was some unknown feeling whose ominous impact compelled a reaction.

"They are a vigilante group. They are enforcing the law by night, issuing justice swiftly and precisely. Reports tell us that the crime rate in Tennessee is falling because of these citizen's efforts. Niggers are beginning to think twice before they accost a white woman, or break in and steal from a white man's home. We are here tonight to organize just such a group, perhaps many groups, here in the low country. To that end, we need money, leadership, and organization. This is why you all were invited here tonight."

Fitz could not believe his ears, was he really sitting here, among Charleston's most influential men, planning a vigilante group to enforce the law? Even if it meant breaking the law? Since when could two wrongs make a right?

The meeting droned on for another hour with proposals, explanations, plans, etc. Finally the Judge said: "At this point, I have someone I want you all to meet. This, ah, gentleman was instrumental in forming and leading one of the most effective Klan groups in Georgia. He has kindly placed his expertise and leadership abilities at our disposal. Gentlemen, Mr. Bobby T. Jordan.

An unshaven man, dressed in a rumpled jacket, ill-fitting

trousers, and riding boots entered the room. On his belt were two revolvers. Sewn to one boot was a leather case from which a nasty looking hunting knife handle projected. But Fitz was mostly captivated by his eyes. They were small, black, and piercing. They burned like two hot coals. One could almost feel the brutality and hatred that radiated from them.

"Thank ya, Judge," he said. Then he placed his hands on his hips and stared around the room, making eye contact with every one present. They lingered momentarily on Fitz.

"In Georgia, we had to kill us a lot o' niggers to make our point and git things goin'. I'm a plain speakin' man, so if any of you pantywaist la-de-das is faint o' heart, we might as well call this thing off right now. This here is serious business and they ain't no room for the daisy folk. The best nigger ah know is the one dangling from a rope. He don't bother nobody, once he stops kickin' and shittin' in his pants. Ya'll want a Klan, I can do it...iffen the price is right. But I has to be in charge. Ya'll jes furnish the money and back off."

Fitz felt a total revulsion for this man. He was brutal white trash with no respect for human life. But the revulsion he felt ran even deeper. So deep that Fitz was at a loss as to why. There was something familiar about him.

Several of the people in the room applauded Jordan's little speech. Others, like Fitz, just sat and stared. Jordan looked around the room once more then said to Judge Lambeau: "I'll be spectin to hear from you along with the money." Then he turned and stalked from the room.

"Gentlemen," the Judge began, "It's time for discussion of the proposal."

One of the men present rose from his chair and said in a loud voice: "you may count on my support, Judge. I pledge one thousand dollars."

Another rose. "I too will pledge one thousand, Your Honor."

Fitz could no help himself. He stood.

"Just a moment. Have you gentlemen given any thought to what we are doing here? Jordan is no law-abiding citizen. This man loves inflicting pain. If he's paid for it, he is even happier. Gentlemen! If we do this we are creating a monster that will, in the end, turn on us and consume it's own benefactors. This is lawlessness Judge Lambeau, I cannot believe you, of all people, would consent to this."

"There is no law, Mr. Manigault!" The judge stood. "We must create some semblance of justice to protect ourselves."

"Your Honor, this is not the answer!" Fitz came back. "We cannot meet lawlessness with lawlessness. That makes us no better than the animals in Columbia and Washington!"

"Then what do you propose, Mr. Manigault? There was anger in the judge's voice.

"I am afraid I have nothing to offer at the moment, Your Honor. But surely there is another way."

"There is no other way!" It was the hotheaded Horace McGill, Jr. "Meet fire with fire I say! I volunteer to head my own claghorn!"

"Here, here!" The room rang with enthusiasm of most of the group.

"This is wrong!" yelled Fitz.

"Get out, Manigault. Go home you panty-waist!" one man yelled.

Fitz looked about the room, shook his head, and left through the door. He could hear the jeers echoing behind him. Just as Fitz stepped outside the door, Jordan stepped in front of him.

"So you're Manigault? I know about you, boy."

For a moment Fitz's mind flashed into the distant past and saw a face grimacing as it jerked Jason up from the river.

"You...it was you that day we had the trouble by the river."

"That's right boy," he laughed. "I ain't through with you Manigaults yet, I see."

"Through with us?"

"You were born with a silver spoon, boy. Ain't never done a day's work in yo' life. I heard you in there running me down."

"Who the hell are you Jordan? Just what is it you want?"

"Just stay out of my way, rich boy."

Fitz was becoming angry. "Then don't make it necessary for me to get in your way. White trash!"

Jordan placed a hand on one of his revolvers and stared into Fitz's eyes. Fitz stared back, cool and unafraid.

"Shoot me and it's murder, Jordan. I'm not armed."

"I could always put the other one by your body, Manigault. Claim you grabbed it and I shot back in self defense." He laughed quietly.

Fitz's eyes grew harder and he tensed his body to strike. Just then the door swung open behind him and several of the more levelheaded men emerged from the meeting.

"Fitz," said one of them, "you're right. This is not the way to handle things, it's just not the thing to do."

Another said, "I'm going home for a hot bath. I feel dirty."

Jordan dropped his hand, turned and disappeared into the night.

For several days Fitz debated about talking to Jason. He knew the church of the Three Crosses was a sore spot with many Charlestonians. It had turned one of Charleston's most prestigious neighborhoods into a "nigger hang-out" where the poor and the wretched, the ignorant and the hopeless, came in droves for food, for shelter and for the promise of a better tomorrow. The Church of the Three Crosses, in any social upheaval of any consequence, would be a primary target. Finally, Fitz decided he had no choice. He sent Jason a message that he would visit the parsonage on Thursday evening.

That Thursday afternoon, before he was to see Jason, a Pinkerton agent called upon him at his office.

"Mr. Manigault, we recently interviewed several old Negroes and a white woman who were on the road between Charleston and the Manigault on the date you gave us. We have reason to believe a gang of cut throats attacked the carriage and killed your friends, then carried your mother off."

"And that's it? I've paid the agency a hundred thousand dollars to tell me the obvious?"

He ignored Fitz. "The gang was traced to Savannah. It's reported that Federal troops killed all but one, the leader, when they attempted to raid an army supply unit. He escaped to Tennessee and was last seen in north Georgia."

Fitz's eyes narrowed. "His name?"

"We don't know, but we think they called him Bobby."

"I see."

"Your instructions, Sir?"

"Continue the investigation, of course. I want to know about my mother!"

"Mr. Manigault, only this "Bobby" character can tell us that. It would be tantamount to a confession, so he is not likely to be forthcoming with information."

"Don't tell me the problems, sir. Bring me answers."

"Yes sir."

"By the way. There is a man presently in Charleston named Bobby T. Jordan. You may wan to consider him a suspect."

The agent's eyes widened. "Do you know this man's whereabouts?"

"No. But Judge Lambeau would."

"Thank you, Mr. Manigault, and good day to you sir."

"Good day."

CHAPTER 31

By the time Fitz reached Jason's that evening, his mother was nowhere in his thoughts. Fitz could consider several subjects in his mind simultaneously. He had that kind of mind. He could also push distractions aside from his thinking and concentrate on the problem at hand. He had that kind of emotional maturity. Since there was nothing he could do but wait to learn more about his mother, he chose not to think of her most of the time.

Mrs. Manly answered the door and left him in the sitting room while she notified Jason of Fitz's arrival. Jason soon entered. Laughing and excited, he embraced his friend and mentor.

Fitz stepped back and took a look at his friend.

"Jason, you look tired. Are you getting any rest?"

"Of course."

"And eating? Are you eating anything?"

"Like a horse, Fitz. Don't worry. I'm fit. I feel fine."

"Maybe you should see a doctor. You've lost weight."

"I'm fine. Now, how can I help you? I pray all the time for an opportunity to repay you in some small way."

"I went to a meeting the other night." They sat down. "A most disturbing meeting."

"The Ku Klux Klan?"

"How did you know?"

"We Negroes may be pretty ignorant as a race right now, but we communicate very well. You'd be surprised how well organized we are, at least at keeping our ears to the ground and each other informed."

"Then you must know the church and schools will be a primary target when trouble comes."

"Yes," Jason said with a sigh. "I'm afraid you're right. It would be a pity, too. Our work is going so well. The Church has the largest congregation in Charleston. The schools and the hospital are running at capacity. We've even almost licked the teacher shortage."

"I don't know how you do it, Jason...running all this."

Jason laughed. "Fitz, you have to be kidding. You're running a multi-national organization. Compared to you, I run very little"

"No. I've dozens of top-notch executives in fifty countries doing the work. I read a few reports and make an occasional decision. That's all."

"Sure it is."

"Honestly. When I look at my organization I see a dozen divisions. When you look at yours you see hundreds of individuals, unique human beings, each one a separate problem."

Jason did not answer.

"But that's enough of that. I've thought about this Klan thing. We can't arm you and your people. We would have a slaughter if you were attacked. Maybe a few dozen security guards?"

"No guns, Fitz! This is God's church, God's schools. There can be no guns here!"

For a moment, Fitz was shocked at the strength of the reaction. But he understood.

"Of course, Jason. But we must do something to protect you and your people."

"I know." Jason sighed and slumped in his chair. "You know, if this thing, this Klan, becomes wide spread, you're a target also?"

"How?"

"You pay an honest day's pay to blacks as well as whites. The whites don't like that."

"True. But a job is worth so much, regardless of the color of the man who does it."

"You've also put a couple of black men in supervisory positions."

"Yes, but they supervise only black gangs."

"Doesn't matter. The whites don't like that either."

"Then they can work some place else."

"You know that's not the issue, Fitz."

"Jason, you're the one avoiding the issue. How are we going to protect the Church of the Three Crosses?"

For a moment there was silence. Then Jason said: "We're going to trust in God and accept his will." The way he said it ended all arguments.

"Alright Jason, whatever you say. But if you change your mind we will do whatever is necessary. Money is not a consideration."

"Fair enough, Fitz. God bless you."

"And you too."

They both rose.

"Give my love to Mary."

"I will."

"You still have a standing invitation to come to our services."

"Thanks, Jason. I think I'll just do that."

As Fitz left the house, Mrs. Manley approached him from the flowerbed where she was working.

"Mr. Manigault."

"Yes, Mrs. Manley?"

"Sir, I'm very concerned about Reverend Apelligo. He is not well. He sleeps very little, he hardly eats enough to keep a cat alive, and recently he passed out right at the dinner table. Oh please don't tell him I told you."

"Thank you, Mrs. Manley. I'll do what I can."

Certainly, Fitz was not surprised. But it hurt him to know his friend was not well.

Jason was a bit surprised when Fitz and Mary appeared in church that Sunday. He was also gratified. They sat close to the front, to Jason's left.

"The church is really beautiful," Mary whispered.

And it was. Fitz looked around him. The walls and ceiling were a stark, but warm, white. The beams, floor and woodwork were a rich mahogany. Real mahogany. Fitz knew it was real because he had dispatched a steamer to bring it from half way around the world. The huge stained-glass windows ran from floor to ceiling, bathing the entire sanctuary in the light of varying hues and colors that seemed to dance and sing praises to God. He also looked at the people. There were a few whites, but mostly they were black. Most were poor, and dressed shabbily. But without exception, they were scrubbed clean with clothes that were as clean as their shining faces. Fitz saw something else that a casual observer would never have seen. It was in their eyes. Their eyes shone with hope, with contentment, with a sense of well being that Judge Lambeau and his bunch could never hope to know.

Just as Jason stood and walked to the pulpit, a cloud slipped from in front of the sun. Jason was suddenly bathed in light as if the sun had focused its energy on that one spot, and placed a diadem upon his head.

Fitz whispered to himself, "This is his son, with whom he is well pleased."

"What dear?" Mary asked softly.

"Nothing, nothing darling."

Jason looked around the room for a long minute, looking into the eyes of all present until every one knew it was he, and he alone to whom Jason would speak.

"My brethren. Our father has blessed us with a beautiful day on which to express our thanks to him for gifts so bountiful that they are beyond counting."

The old blacks present looked down and shook their heads nodding their appreciation. The young ones looked up toward Jason, seeming to absorb the love of God that emanated from this frail man. Fitz was enthralled. Never had he dreamed of the charisma his long time friend was exuding.

"He came. And he walked among us. He broke bread with us. He healed so many of us. He wept for us. He lay down his life for us.

Can you think on these things of our Lord Jesus Christ and still call yourself 'nigger'? Think of yourself as unworthy? Think of yourself as stupid? Undeserving? Of course you do. And of course you are! But not in the sight of God. Only in the sight of man. So rejoice that God loves you, accepts you, cares for you. And work so that the white man will gain respect and allow you your proper place in the brotherhood of man. When I say work, I don't mean load more barges, plow more cotton, or cook more meals. I mean learn, learn, learn! Learn to read. Learn a trade so that you can feed yourself and your family. Become so important to our community that you are needed for your mind as well as for your back. This will not be a simple task. At this very moment, there are those who are organizing and gaining strength that would rather see us dead as animals, than alive as men. They will come, and they will have their day. But we will not be beaten. Someday we will prevail and find our place. But I tell you, here and now, not one of us in this room will live to see that day. But it will come. The day will come when black men and white men will stand side by side as equals to do the work of God. But God will not just hand us that day. We must work for it. We must learn. We cannot fight for that day, we cannot kill for that day, and we cannot just wait for that day. We must work! Work! Work! And we must give. Give of ourselves. To each other and to God. To everyone in need no matter what the color of his or her skin.

Jason paused for what seemed like minutes.

"There is one among us that I would have you all know." He looked at Fitz. "Mr. Manigault, would you please stand."

Fitz, somewhat embarrassed and puzzled, rose to his feet.

"I want everyone here to take a close look at this man. Remember his face. And remember his name–Manigault. Without him, this church would not be standing. Without him there would be no school here. No hospital. Without him, you who are sitting here with full bellies and clothes on you back would be starving and naked. You would be digging roots and hiding behind pine boughs without him. Remember his face. Remember his name. Manigault! I would die for this man. I expect no less from each of you. This white man is a hundred years ahead of his time and unlike any other white man you may ever know. He has, in his way, given us these things without asking anything in return. I pledge my life and I pledge the lives of all of you to his welfare. Anytime, anywhere, this man needs help, I expect you to see he gets it–no matter what the cost."

The room was totally silent when Jason stopped. He looked again from eye to eye. They understood what Jason had said. Fitz realized Jason had just pledged hundreds of black men to his, and his family's, protection. Even though Jason and the Church of the Three Crosses would have to meet whatever destruction may come along, Fitz would now be watched over by every God-fearing Negro in the low country of South Carolina. Fitz held a new respect for Jason's power.

On the walk home, Fitz said, "Mary, I thought I was a man of influence and power, but Jason has me beaten. He wields more power than I can imagine. I buy my way with money. He has captured the hearts of everyone with his words and his good work. They really love him.

"They love you too, Fitz. Without you, Jason could have done very little."

"You know, I doubt that very much. He would have succeeded without me. I'm very glad that I have been used in all this. But Jason would have found a way without my help."

But Jason's influence and fame far exceeded even what Fitz believed. Throughout South Carolina, throughout the South, even to the far reaches of New England, Negroes were spreading the fame of the Church of the Three Crosses and its minister, the giving, loving Reverend Apelligo. Black men and women were walking hundreds of miles to learn at Jason's feet and find fair wages with Manigault Shipping, which now had huge operations in Charleston, Savannah, Georgetown, Beaufort, Columbia and Lancaster. Jason had shaped his schools to provide Manigault Shipping with skilled workers. Fitz had supported, and welcomed, this feeder to his labor pool. A graduate of the school of the Church of the Three Crosses had no fear of not finding a job. Manigault Shipping, on the other hand, could be confident that such a man would be an excellent worker.

They, Manigault Shipping and the church school, complimented each other perfectly. This was no secret. Even Bobby T. Jordan knew it. Then too, Jason's effort to organize the southern Negro churches was having a tremendous impact. The once frail, individual congregations were taking heart in the fact that there were many others with them and that Jason and the Church of the Three Crosses, the richest, largest, and most powerful church of them all, would watch over them.

CHAPTER 32

It was a bleak, rainy, dark afternoon. Far out to sea off the coast of the Carolinas, a hurricane raged on in its slow northward trek. In Judge Lambeau's home, another sinister storm was also brewing.

"I got ovah a hunert men organized and ready," Jordan said to the Judge. "We can rule the low country any time you give the word."

Judge Lambeau and Horace McGill sat sipping sherry as Bobby T. brought them up to date on his organizational efforts. Judge Lambeau was visibly uncomfortable with Jordan and with his attitude. Even the impetuous Horace McGill could feel a sense of fear toward the Klan and its aims. But both men could see no alternative to restoring some of their version of justice and safety to their homeland.

As for Bobby T., he was practically salivating over his new position. Soon he would be the most powerful man in the low country with a veritable army of white trash at his command. This would be so much more lucrative than Tennessee or North Georgia. Even though Yankee troops, carpetbaggers, and scallywags had raped the once rich low country, there was still plenty for the taking.

"Now that's the organization," Bobby T. began. "Next is our operations. We need to start out big, git everybody's attention. Our first target is the niggah church on Lambol Street. We gonna learn everybody that teachin' a niggah to read don't pay. First thing you know, we gonna drown in uppity niggahs. Soon as we burn that damn place to the ground, we gonna hit the niggah lovers who keep it goin'. That means Manigault Shippin'. He'll be giving his last niggah a job when white folks is out o' work."

"But that could destroy what little economy we have!" blurted the judge, spilling his sherry.

"You mean the niggah economy?"

"No. Manigault Shipping is our biggest employer. All the shipping in the state terminates in Charleston. No! No! We can't destroy Manigault Shipping. I'll reason with Fitzsimmons Manigault. We'll get him on our side. You leave him alone."

"Judge, when I finish with that niggah church, they ain't gonna be no reasonin' with yo' niggah lover."

"That's true, Judge," said McGill.

"Then we can't bother the church!" the Judge shouted adamantly. We'll have to start some place else, in some other way and then see how things develop."

"Like what?" Bobby T. asked, obviously angry.

"Well," said McGill, coming to the Judge's rescue, "the Pettigrew Plantation has been taken over by the Negroes. Why don't you go out there and run them out?"

Bobby T. thought for a moment. He wanted Manigault! But he didn't want to lose the respectability the Judge gave his venture. He would play along, he decided. It was much too early for him to play his full hand.

"Awright, sir," he said like a true subordinate. "If that's what you gentlemen want, you is the bosses. I'll clean up the Pettigrew situation. That should start the word gittin' round."

"Yes," said the Judge, relieved. "And I do wish you would keep bloodshed to a minimum. We just want to scare them back into line."

"Of course, Judge." Bobby T. smiled, his rotten teeth stained yellow. "We don't want to hurt nobody."

Life was different on the Pettigrew plantation, as it was everywhere in the South. The plantation had been abandoned by its mistress. Her husband had been killed in the early stages of the war.

After Appomattox, she had returned to Philadelphia to her mother and father. But before she left, she called her loyal Negroes together for a farewell meeting.

"James," she said to the her butler, "I leave the Pettigrew in your care. It is yours, and your children's and your children's children in perpetuity for all times. I am sorry to leave you. You were faithful to me, but I cannot go on alone. With God's help, you will all be all right. May he help you to prosper."

Then she had gone. There were no deeds, no documents; nothing was recorded. It had only been her wish. Her words had barely finished echoing when rumor had begun that the Negroes had run her off and taken over the Pettigrew plantation. This rumor, to the casual observer, would have appeared to be correct. James and the several other loyal blacks turned no one in need away, but welcomed them to stay and work and partake of the Pettigrew's successes and failures.

By the time Bobby T. chose the Pettigrew as an example to all 'uppidy niggahs', there were over a hundred black women and children working and living there. Even though the government had not yet foreclosed for back taxes, that too would soon be a reality.

The night was almost as bright as day when sixty Klansmen reined up at the entrance to the Pettigrew plantation house. The hurricane had moved away and the weather behind it shone a billion stars and a full, glowing moon. Nevertheless, when they lit their torches and came galloping up the lane, screaming and shouting, they brought even more light to the night. It was over quickly. In twenty minutes, thirty-one bodies littered the ground. Most were dead, the others dying. Some had been shot, some hacked to death with swords, some trampled by the hysterical horses. The rest were pressed into a circle to stand and watch while every building was torched. They saved the main house for last. Then in its raging fiery glow, they hung James and the others.

The voice of the leader rang out above the weeping of the survivors and the crackling flames. "We'll be back tomorrow! If they's one of you still here, he'll be a dead niggah!"

They threw down their torches and rode away, this time silently, into the night.

It was Jason who brought the news to Fitz.

"All the survivors came to the church. The doctor has seen to them and we've found everyone a place to sleep."

Fitz looked out his window across a harbor bustling with Manigault ships.

"Then it has begun," Fitz said. "I had hoped they would think better of this."

"They were brutal. Absolutely no regard for life, much less property. It was out and out murder. A carnage."

Fitz sighed deeply. "I suppose this was to be some kind of lesson. But all I can read in it is hate. Evil unleashed. And unleashed by good men, I'm afraid."

"Why the Pettigrew place? Why not the Church of the Three Crosses?"

"I don't know, but they'll work up to you I'm sure."

"No doubt."

"I'm going to hire you a security force, Jason. We'll need about fifty good men–good shots. I'll..."

"No! My God, Fitz, we can't be like them."

Fitz looked at him wide-eyed. "For God's sake, you're the number one target in the state. Killing you would be a coup for any one of them. What the hell do you mean by 'no'?"

"I won't see a man, much less men, being killed to spare my life."

"Well I will."

"I won't allow it. Violence breeds violence! I'll not do it!"

"Then you're a walking dead man, my old friend."

"So be it."

"I don't understand you, Jason. You've done more to help put the South back together than any man I know, yet you're just willing to give up, lie down and die. Don't you think God might expect a little fight out of you? Martyrs we don't need! All the dead saints put together aren't going to help your people. It's up to you! But first, you have to survive!"

For a moment, Fitz's logic overwhelmed Jason. He had no answer.

"Besides, it's my decision, not yours. I have to protect my investment."

"You can't call it an investment. It has cost you millions of dollars and you've never gotten a dime back, and never will I'm afraid."

"That's absurd, Jason. All right, I have invested hundreds of thousands in the church and its work. The return at the moment is a hundred million. If you want to talk money, God has blessed me beyond all measure. I believe that you and the Church of the Three Crosses are at the bottom of that."

"I never could argue with you. You always blow me out of the water. All right, do whatever you want. You'll do it anyway."

Thank you, Jason. I appreciate your permission."

"Now you really have a problem. Where are you going to get fifty men to protect a Negro church?"

"The Pinkerton Agency, of course."

It took three weeks for the Pinkerton men to appear. Jason had hated the thought of uniformed, armed guards swarming over the church and school grounds. It was not like that at all. The guards blended in as gardeners, repairmen, and maintenance people. With their weapons concealed, they were inconspicuous. A hastily constructed barracks blended with the other buildings and drew no attention. But, of course, this was good only from the perspective of how things looked. The entire community soon knew of their presence. That included Bobby T. Jordan and his claghorn.

"That's fine," said Fitz to Jason. "It should help discourage any thought of attacking the church."

"Perhaps, but meanwhile the hangings, shootings and burnings are going on all over. Surely there must be some way to stop it."

"I'm afraid not, Jason. The tiger is out of his cage. The men who let him out are now helpless to stop him, though I doubt they know that yet."

Not a night passed that the Klan did not ride. Old scores were being settled. Killings were done for profit. There were dozens of reasons, all in the name of 'restoring order'. Judge Lambeau and his inner circle became more and more nervous as their lack of control over Bobby T. and his organization became more obvious.

"I believe," said the judge to Horace McGill and six of the other backers gathered in his home. "It is time we called in Mr. Jordan and redefined our goals and the means to those ends that we will tolerate."

The gathering was in agreement.

"Horace, did you get the message to him?"

"I did, Judge. He should be along shortly."

The door opened without a knock. Jordan strode in, sat, and threw his feet up on the Judge's desk. His spurs dug deeply into the highly polished surface. He was dressed much differently than before. Now he wore all black, his mother of pearl buttons encased in silver. His gun belt and boots were highly polished and richly embossed.

"Kindly remove your feet from my grandfather's desk, Mr. Jordan."

Jordan met the Judge's enraged stare with cool, calculated hatred in his eyes. Slowly, dragging the spurs, he put his feet on the floor.

It took a moment for the judge to contain himself.

"Jordan." This time he did not say mister. "We called you here to tell you there is too much killing. Too much property damage. And we don't understand all the stealing that's going on..."

"Now jest a minute. You talkin' 'bout all them copycat outfits. Now can I help it ifin some farmer's got a score to settle, he wears a sheet to do it? Or if some red neck puts on a sheet to rob somebody?"

"Don't lie to us, Jordan. Those people don't ride with thirty to a hundred men.'"

"Shut up!" Jordan yelled as he stood to his feet.

The judge, aghast, sat back in his chair. Throughout the room there was silence.

The work of the Klan ain't none of yo' business. I ain't gonna listen to any mo' of yo' mealy mouths. Bobby T. is in charge of the Klan and they'll do as I say. Understand?"

The judge had resigned himself. "In that case we have no choice but to withdraw our financial support and put you out of business."

Bobby T. roared with laughter. "You ain't gonna do no such thang, Judge.

"The hell we won't!" Horace stood.

"Set down, boy, or I'll blow you setter off."

Horace sat.

"Hit would be a shame iffen the Klan decided you gentlemens was niggah lovers, now wouldn't it? You stop yo' money and I reckon that's the onliest thang they could believe. Now ain't it? I recken ya'll jest better do like you been doin' and leave the thinking to me. It would be a shame, Judge, iffen somebody hung you in yo' perty little garden out there and burned this fancy house to the ground. Git my meanin'?"

He rose and left the room without another word. His laughter trailed behind him.

So now they knew. They were in control of nothing. Just subject to the same violence and carnage to which they had subjected the entire countryside.

In Jordan's heart burned the need for the final revenge against the Manigaults. Fitz was the only surviving member. Only his death would satisfy Jordan for the humiliation he had suffered that day on the riverbank and, to a much lesser degree, his brother's death. Destroying Fitz had become an obsession. It had become an act he looked forward to. So much so that he was in no hurry. He liked thinking about it, letting the hatred build. Hell, that was half the fun. Once it was over, he would have to focus his hate somewhere else and that may not be as much fun. He was in no hurry. The judge had done him a favor; he had sustained the fires of hate.

For the next few weeks, the Klan increased its tempo. When night fell the blacks locked their doors and shutters and remained in their homes, dreading the sound of approaching horsemen. Very little of the Klan's activities were conducted within the confines of the city. Mostly, they were far afield in the remote areas of the farms and plantations. However, it was not unheard of. Occasionally, people were abducted and hanged in the heart of the city. The city would awaken to find the results of the Klan's presence. Sometimes, they were shot from ambush, or a home was torched. Sometimes they were hanged on a prominent oak in town, but mostly the Klan worked the rural areas. Federal troops made an effort to catch them, but to no avail. The Yankees did not know the countryside and they could never hope to get any help from the populace. In so far as the local law was concerned, no one knew just how many of them were Clan members. They were ineffective either through ineptitude or on purpose. So the Klan rode, for all purposes, unopposed. As their power grew, so did their corruption. Soon Jordan knew that even his influence over the Klan was limited. He took steps to secure his position so that, at least for a while, his attention was turned away from Fitz and to the purges within the Klan structure. This would be, he decided, an on-going process, for there would always be those who lusted for his power, position, and ever-growing wealth.

CHAPTER 33

Mrs. Manly had finished serving tea to the five distinguished looking Negroes who had come calling on Jason.

"Will there be anything further, Reverend Apelligo?"

"No, thank you. I'll call you if we need you."

She left. Reverend Franklin, smiling broadly, said, "The convention was a tremendous success. Your many hours of hard work have truly paid tremendous dividends. And, of course, it is your endorsement that has guaranteed our success. We had only to mention your name and the other churches flocked to us during the earlier organizational phases.

"I'm sorry I have not been able to play a more active role in the work, but I've been so busy here, getting away was just totally impossible. I apologize for missing the first convention. I understand churches from Virginia to Louisiana were represented."

"That's true. Every southern state, and some of the border states too."

"That's gratifying."

The men looked from one to another with puzzled expressions. After a long silence, the Reverend Franklin said, "Sir, didn't you get the convention's letter?"

"I...I'm afraid not."

"I see. Well, sir, no wonder for the awkwardness of the situation. First, we are the officers the convention has newly appointed to head the Diocese we formed."

"That's wonderful, Matthew, John, Frederick, William, James..." They looked at him as he named them each in turn.

"Thank you. Now, the convention has named the Diocese 'The Church of the Southern Cross'. They appointed us Secretary, Treasurer, Director of Christian Affairs, Director of expansion..." He pointed to each man in turn as he announced his title. "And myself as senior director and first assistant to the Bishop." He stopped and looked at Jason expectantly.

Jason aware of the expectation in his face said, "Go on, Matthew."

"The convention selected Charleston as our headquarters."

"Oh, that was wise. Charleston is an apt place for it."

"And the Church of the Three Crosses is the Mother church."

Jason reacted as his mind began to put the picture together. "I had not realized that...I thought, perhaps...I'm not sure we have the facilities for a regional headquarters here. And what about the Bishop of the Diocese? He'll need a place. Perhaps the parsonage. I could move to the dormitory..." Jason was thinking out loud.

"Sir," Franklin held up his hand, "I apologize. It has not been our intent to play a game with you, but it would seem we have been doing just that. Reverend Apelligo, I've been empowered, by unanimous vote of the convention of the Church of the Southern cross, to inform you that, as of noon this Sunday, you are Bishop Jason Apelligo, First Bishop and absolute church leader of the one hundred and thirty-eight thousand members of the Church of the Southern Cross. May God bless you in every way."

The entire group rose to their feet and applauded.

Jason sat dumbfounded. He had not dreamed he, so young, would be appointed Bishop.

"At least, those were the figures a month ago. Churches are joining every day. No telling what the count is now. I..."

"Me? I am the Bishop? But why? I..."

"Yes sir, you are the Bishop. The first black Bishop and, most assuredly, the greatest. As to why, surely the Bishop must know that he is the most famous and revered black Christian leader on the continent."

Suddenly, Jason stood.

"Mrs. Manly! Mrs. Manly!"

"Yes, Reverend Apelligo?" She appeared instantly.

"Would you be kind enough to bring us some sherry, Mrs. Manly?"

"Of course." She left to fetch it.

Fitz had heard the news days before the church officers had arrived in Charleston. But he had said nothing, preferring that Jason be informed by his own people in their own way. By the time Jason knew, the entire South knew. In spite of everything, Charleston felt a sense of pride that the massive Negro Christian movement had chosen on of Charleston's own to lead it. As soon as he knew Jason had been informed, Fitz rushed to congratulate him.

"I'm still in shock, Fitz. Can't seem to focus my mind. This presents me with so many problems. How can I run the Church of the Three Crosses and standardize and direct several hundred other churches as well? There's so little time in a day as it is."

"Organization, Jason. Of course you can't carry a load like that alone. I'll help you. This is my cup of tea."

"Fitz, I can't continue to call on you for everything..."

"Haven't we been through this before? First thing we need to do is create an organizational chart that will insure all the needs of the church are found, addressed, and under competent supervision while they're being met. Then we need to find the right men to fill the positions. And, by God, I believe you've already done that. Once they're operating, it's simply a matter of supervising the top layer, letting the top layer supervise the lower layers, and so forth."

"We're back to the same old two problems again, Fitz. Money and qualified people. We're talking about large numbers here. But there is no money. Most of the churches can barely feed their own ministers."

"Money is no problem, and there are qualified people out there. You can find them."

"I can't continue letting you stuff vast sums of money into my career, I..."

"I'll give the new organization one million dollars to get going. Your staff can ride Manigault trains and ships for free. There will be a lot of traveling, you know. We have to find you some office space separate from your work here. And there's..."

"Fitz, you're not listening to me again. Did you hear what I said?"

"Jason, don't deny me this, please!"

Fitz looked into his eyes and Jason knew he was sincere. There was more to this than even friendship. Fitz served God in his own way. This was his way.

"I hope I'm not rationalizing. But you make it difficult to say no. I...deep in my heart...I really believe your helping my people is God's calling for you." He sighed heavily. "How can I interfere between the two of you–God almighty and the finest human being I have ever known.

"Great, little brother. Now let's go to work."

They worked all night organizing the newly formed Diocese of the Church of the Southern Cross. As the night began to lighten with the rising sun, Fitz was still animated and excited over their work. He stopped short, however, when the sun streamed through he window and fell upon Jason.

"What's wrong, Jason?"

Jason's breathing had become labored. His eyes, far back in his head, shone with pain.

"Just a little tired. I'm not used to these hours."

"My God, I've kept you up all night! I'm sorry, friend. I guess I got a little carried away."

"Don't be sorry. We've done a weeks work in a few hours. I am beholden to you. I am, and always will be, beholden to you."

"You had best go to bed, Jason. And so had I. I am so stupid to do this to you! Go to bed. I'm leaving."

But Jason did no go to bed after Fitz left. He leaned back in his chair, tears streaming down his face from the pain that rippled through his chest. It was eight o'clock when Mrs. Manly found him sleeping peacefully, still in his chair.

CHAPTER 34

"*Have you heard about that fancy doo-dad nigger bein' a bishop,* Bobby T?" asked one of Jordan's lieutenants.

"Yeah, I heard."

"Then how come he's still livin'? That damn bunch of his has niggers all over the place down yonder on Lambol. It ain't safe for a white man to be down there no more. I swear to God, these worthless niggers is takin' over the best parts of Charleston and you jest sittin' back on your ass an' lettin' 'em."

Bobby T. came out of his chair and grabbed him by the throat. He said in almost a whisper, "Now you listen to me, you son of a bitch, Bobby T. does things his way in his own good time. Don't you ever question me again. Ever! Or I'll feed you to the dawgs."

The truth is that Jason's new fame had him planning and plotting anew. Bobby T. knew that the best way to end Jason and his church was to cut off its life's blood. That was Fitz. But he could not be sure Fitz had not provided for the church in his estate. Were that true, he would have to destroy them both after all. Under the right circumstances, either could survive without the other. He needed to destroy them both. Swiftly, and finally. He had been planning it for days.

⋅⊰⋅✠⋅⊱⋅

A month later, Fitz hailed Jason in the churchyard. "Jason, do you have a minute?"

"I owe you my life, Fitz. I can certainly give you a minute."

"I have to run up to Norfolk on business on Thursday. I thought you might want to come along and visit your regional office in Raleigh. Mary's going with me. We could drop you off on the way up and pick you up on the way back."

"On Thursday?"

"Yes. We'll be gone three weeks."

"I can't Fitz. The Diocese has called a meeting of all regional directors for next week. I have to be here."

"Of course. I understand. Well, perhaps next time."

"Thank you Fitz, for thinking of me. I hope it can be next time."

Fitz and Mary left for Norfolk in their private train car on schedule. He was routed straight through, no stops. At the last minute, Aunt Catherine had agreed to go with them. She did not like to leave Charleston, even for a few days. But Fitz and Mary had worn her down. So, she consented. She passed out her orders with her usual vigor.

"Now, Abraham, even though I'm not here, I still want fresh flowers in the house every day."

"Yes, Ma'am."

"And you see to my cat, you hear?"

"Yes, Ma'am. Don't you worry. We'll take real good care of her."

"And keep her away from that nasty tomcat that's been coming round here."

"Yes, Ma'am."

"Well, I can't think of anything else. You will all be fine, I'm sure."

"Yes, Ma'am."

When Fitz, Mary, and Catherine left for Norfolk, there was no slackening of the work at the house. Meta and Abraham would continue to shine and polish and maintain everything in sight. Of the remnants of the original Manigault slaves Catherine had taken in only four remained, beside Meta and Abraham. They were old and fragile. Nevertheless they kept the grounds in impeccable order. The yard was small, so a lot of work was not necessary. Mostly, they sat in the sun and warmed their tired, old bones. Everyone at the house tried to make sure they didn't overdo.

It will be a continuing mystery that Jordan never learned of Fitz's departure for Norfolk. Had he known, he most surely would have postponed his plans. But, in his ignorance, the raid went on as scheduled. It was a simple plan, and a deadly one.

The Klan would mount a two-pronged attack. Twenty men would attack Catherine's house. The rest, something in the neighborhood of a hundred, would simultaneously attack the church. This would, at least should, establish the Klan's supremacy in the low country with no remaining doubt. At least, it would in Jordan's mind.

Bobby T. chose to lead the raid on the house. He did this for two reasons. The reason he gave his lieutenants was his desire to personally dispatch Fitz, which was true. The reason he did not mention was the armed and trained security force that defended the church grounds. The orders were simple. Kill everyone, burn everything. Then, disperse and do not meet again until summoned. Bobby T. knew such a massacre was going to bring tremendous repercussions from the local citizens, Columbia, and even Washington D.C. This would make, or break, the South Carolina Klan. He never mentioned the possibility of his having to flee the South. But he knew he might have to because of the Pinkerton men. He turned everything into cash in the event flight became necessary. In many ways, he was a cautious man.

Bobby T knew the raids were foolhardy, but his burning hate for the Manigaults, plus the external pressure to do something about the church, had put him in a corner.

CHAPTER 35

It was a typical autumn night in Charleston. The humidity was soaring, the temperatures high. The only hint that winter was coming was a breeze that somewhat freshened the air and blew the stench of the marsh out to sea. Individual riders, and pairs, came by way of Meeting Street, up to Rutledge and Ashley Avenues, down Broad, past the corner of the Four Justices, and through he various alleys. They quietly assembled two blocks from Lambol. Only the snorting of the horses and their occasional pawing at the cobblestones could be heard as the hundred and twelve men donned their sheets and hoods.

At that same moment, Bobby T. and his twenty handpicked men were assembling off the battery, just two hundred yards from the house.

On Lambol, at a signal, the horsemen lined up four abreast and started up the street. A hundred yards from the church, they stopped, and on a second signal, a hundred and twelve torches were lighted. The burning torches turned the night into day. Around them, the shadows of the trees danced across the colonnades of the majestic homes that once were occupied by fine old families, now stood empty and rotting because of the church's presence. An alert guard at the church was instantly aware of them. He grabbed a rope and jerked repeatedly. In the security forces barracks, a bell rang excitedly.

"This is it!" bellowed the half-asleep officer in charge. "To your stations! Move!"

They poured from the barracks in every direction. The designated men rushed to the dormitories and hospital to waken the blacks and help them to cover. In the parsonage, Mrs. Manly shook Jason awake and literally began to drag him towards the wet and moldy old basement.

"I don't care what you say, your Grace. Mr. Manigault left explicit instructions, as did the Captain of the Guard."

Screaming their blood-curdling Rebel yell, the horsemen came galloping up the street. The horses were first to pick up the hysteria that was building. Nostrils flaring, eyes ablaze, some panicked and threw the well-disciplined column into chaos. At that moment, the rooftops sparkled with gunfire as a Pinkerton gatlin gun poured shot into the advancing formation. Seventeen riders were blown from their saddles instantly. Horses crumpled from the impact of the lead pellets. But they came on. By now, all the guards were in position. Their first volley threw the riders into even more confusion. The formation broke and individual groups swarmed onto the church grounds, firing repeatedly at the muzzle flashes, the shadows, any movement at all. Torches were thrown at random towards the rooftops and through the windows. The hail of bullets from the security force continued to take its toll as the guards began firing on individual riders. They were all excellent shots and seasoned combat veterans. There were, in fact, very few inept Pinkerton men. Wherever those few were, they were not at the church tonight.

The hospital roof erupted in flames as a torch thrown into a linen closet did its job. Fires sprang from one dormitory, a window of the school, and from behind a shattered stained glass window in the sanctuary. The security guard continued to rain accurate, merciless hails of bullets down on the Klansmen. First one, then another, spun his mount and headed for the safety of the open road. In minutes, they had all panicked, and fled. Silence, except for the crackling of the flames and the moans of the dieing, engulfed the church grounds.

Meanwhile, on the Battery, twenty-one men had left the cover of the nearby trees and swarmed over the grounds of the house.

Several slipped into the carriage house and bludgeoned or slit the throats of the four old sleeping Negroes.

Kicking the door down, Bobby T., and a dozen men rushed into the house, scattering to search the rooms. Bobby remained in the foyer, nervously watching in the event Fitz confronted him. Two men began lighting lamps so they could watch the fun when Fitz was dragged down the stairs. But the men who had searched the bedrooms returned empty handed, except for some of Mary's jewelry and several pieces of the fine linens they had stumbled upon.

"He ain't up there, Bobby T. We done looked under the beds, in the wardrobes...everywhere. He ain't here!"

At that moment, the men who had searched the servants' quarters on the basement floor, entered with Meta and Abraham. Abraham was dazed and bleeding from the scalp. Meta was wide-eyed with terror. Blood trickled from the corner of her mouth and one eye was already swelling shut.

"Where is yo' master, nigga?" Bobby T. roared at Abraham.

Abraham stared into his eyes and said nothing.

"Did you hear me, nigga? Where's Manigault?"

Abraham continued his cold, unrelenting stare. "I am a free man. Get out of this house!"

"Put him on his knees," Bobby T. hissed. "No nigga talks to me like that."

The two men forced Abraham to his knees, almost wrenching his arms from their sockets in the process. Bobby T. stepped behind him and placed the muzzle of this pistol against the back of Abraham's head.

"One more chance, nigga. Where is he?"

"You can go to hell, white trash."

The 44-caliber bullet blew out Abraham's entire face, splattering blood and gray matter over the fine oriental carpet. Meta's scream pierced the night and dissolved into sobbing.

"Yo' turn, nigga bitch. Where is Manigault?"

"He ain't here. He gone to Norfolk," said Meta with her whole body jerking with her sobs.

"God damn it?" Bobby T. spat. "Kill her!" he shouted to the man holding her. He pulled his knife, plunged it into her belly and jerked upward and out, disemboweling her.

At that instant shooting rang out in the yard. A man yelled through the door.

"It's the Pinkerton's from the church. Some of 'ems comin' here!"

When things had quieted down at the church, the guards and the residents had begun fighting fires and evacuating the buildings. Jason had gotten away from Mrs. Manly and rushed onto the grounds just as the raiders were leaving. Fearing the worst, he grabbed half a dozen men and started for Fitz's house on foot. The Pinkerton men had opened fire while still coming up the street. Jason, though leading the charge, was unarmed.

"Burn it!" yelled Bobby T. as he ran trough the open door and into the safety of the night. The two men lit their torches. One threw his up the stairs into a bedroom. The other tossed his into the library where it landed on a sofa. The two men started for the door but were cut down by the relief force rushing up the front walk. Jason and his people rushed into the house. Two of the men dashed up the stairs and into the library to put out the burning sofa.

Jason stared in horror at his parents. Abraham was dead. There was no identifying him, but Jason knew it was Abraham. Meta, eyes glazed with pain that was unimaginable, took great comfort in seeing her son alive. Jason, and the guard with him, picked her up and carried her from the smoke-filled room to the front lawn.

"Mama!" Jason cried as he cradled her head in his arms.

"My son, the Bishop," she said with a smile.

"For God's sake," Jason yelled to the guard, "get a doctor, now!

The guard left at a dead run for the hospital, which at that moment was being consumed in flames.

"Hang on, Mama. We'll get you some help soon."

Meta's breathing was labored. The pain drove her out of consciousness and back again in pulses. She clutched her son tightly in a more lucid moment. Then she looked into his eyes and wiped a tear from his cheek.

Don't grieve for me, Jason. You have brought me pride and joy beyond any mother's wildest dreams. My son, the Bishop. My son, the giver of love and kindness. Her fingers tightened and bit into his bare arms. Her breath raced through her teeth until the pain subsided once more.

"Jason, there is something I must tell you before I die."

"Please don't talk Mama. It makes the bleeding worse."

"But I must, I have a heavy burden that I must lay down before I go." Again her entire body tightened as the pain pulsated through her.

"Hang on, Mama. Please hang on!"

I was once a very beautiful girl, Jason. Statuesque. That's what Fitzsimmons called me, statuesque. It took me a long time to be able to say it, and to know what it meant, but I knew it was good.

Jason could see the doctor and several guards running up the battery toward them.

"Mama, the doctor is coming now."

"The pain is gone, Jason. I must hurry. Fitzsimmons Manigault senior was your father. You've some fine blood in your veins, son. It has shone, too, hasn't it? I want your forgiveness. Abraham forgave me long ago. Now I need yours."

"Hush, Mama. The doctor is here."

"No. Please, Jason. Say you forgive me. Please!"

The doctor knelt and examined the wound. Meta screamed as he attempted to push her intestines back into the cavity. She fainted.

We must get her somewhere I can see to stop the bleeding. She's bleeding to death. She's cold, probably in shock."

Jason started to pick her up.

"No! We need a wagon. Carrying her will kill her."

He stooped again and took her pulse. Then he knelt and put his ear to her chest, which no longer heaved. He stood slowly.

"I'm sorry, your Grace. It is done. We were too late and her injury was too severe.

Jason looked at the doctor for a long moment. Then he rose,

turned, and slowly walked to the railing on the seawall across the street. Gripping it tightly, he stared out into the vastness, where he noticed that the glow of the moon danced on the water into seeming infinity.

He looked up and prayed: "We are so fragile, dear Father. You are so strong. Yet it is we who must bare the pain of this world. You sit in your Holy Temple, immune to heat, to cold, to vengeance, to physical and emotional pain, yet you shower these things, and a thousand evils like them, upon us!" Suddenly he threw his hands up and screamed at the top of his lungs, "Do you know how it feels? Is this all a joke? Are you bored up there? Does our suffering amuse you? What would you have of us? Explain yourself!"

Then he bowed is head. Suddenly, he looked up. He turned and ran back to where Meta was still lying. Dropping down beside her, he took her lifeless body into his arms and, rocking back and forth, said: "I forgive you Mama. I forgive you. Mama, please come back! Wake up, Mama!"

He began to try to shake her awake. "Please wake up!"

The doctor and a guard pried his grip from her.

"Come with me, your Grace. We must get you home."

Jason went limp. He awoke in bed. Mrs. Manly was wiping his forehead with a cold towel.

"You'll be fine, your Grace. You've been asleep for hours."

"What time is it?"

"Three o'clock in the afternoon."

Jason sat up with a start. Then the impact of the previous night hit him.

"My God!! Mrs. Manly, what has happened? How many dead? How much damage? I'm needed…He tried to get up.

"Just stay exactly where you are, your Grace. There's plenty of time. They're already cleaning up the mess."

"How many dead?"

"Seven of the hospital patients. They couldn't get them out in time."

"Only seven?"

"Well, there were sixty-three Klan bodies. I must say Mr. Manigault's security forces are excellent at what they do."

"My mother, my father?"

"They're in the sanctuary, your Grace. I am so sorry."

"How many dead at the house?"

"All of them, I'm afraid. All six. There were two Klan bodies there."

"And the damages?"

"The hospital is gone. There is some damage to the main dormitory. One bedroom, actually. The sanctuary has a broken window and three of the pews are scorched."

"And at Fitz's?"

"The carriage house and a little damage in the house."

"I see."

"We were lucky, your Grace, except for the people."

"Yes, except for the people."

CHAPTER 36

Bobby T. paced back and forth in his cabin. He was in a rage.
Two of his lieutenants listened uncomfortably.

"Of all the damn stupid moves I ever heard tell of! You dumb bastards jest paraded up the street with torches all lit up and..."

He slammed his fist into the table as he sat down and poured another drink.

"We is finished around here!" I won't be able to git a dozen riders after this! Sixty-five dead, twenty more wounded. You damn stupid idiots!"

"What we gonna do, Bobby T.?" asked one of the men.

"I'm gittin' the hell out of this part of the country. I don't give a damn what you do. Damn it! You fools didn't do yo' job! We missed Manigault. We done almost no damage. You let them bastards break your backs! Why didn't you find out Manigault was gone? Answer me, Barnwell!"

"It couldn't be helped. I was busy gittin' the men together. He ain't never left town before. He's always home, every night. Like clockwork.

"And you Taylor! You dumb bastard! Where the hell did you learn tactics? On a wagon train?"

Taylor shrugged. "Now damn it. You never said nothin' bout no gatlin gun."

"I can't know ever'thing! I ought to shoot the both of you! Don't you understand? We could have ruled this whole country. Now we got to run and hide like rats!"

Taylor became visibly angry. He had taken enough abuse.

"Tell me this Bobby T., iffen you so damn smart, how come you didn't take on that security force yoself? Yeller? Is..."

The pistol ball lifted Taylor from his chair and slammed him against the wall. He never knew what hit him.

"Keep yo' hans on the table, Barnwell," said Bobby T. as he trained the muzzle of his weapon between his eyes.

"Now be calm, Bobby T." He looked nervously at Taylor's limp body. "I'm glad yo done it. He was plannin' to take yo' place. I was gonna tell you, or just kill him myself."

"Yeah? I'll just bet you wuz."

The bone shattering impact of the bullet against Barnwell's skull was louder than the pistol's report. Bobby T. holstered his weapon, grabbed his saddlebags and left the cabin. Only minutes after he galloped into the forest, a Pinkerton man and half a dozen deputies reined up and stormed the cabin. They received no resistance from the staring bodies inside.

"We're too late," yelled one of the deputies as he emerged for the house. "He's not here."

"Do you think he found out we were coming?"

"I doubt it. But we'll get him. He'll crop up somewhere. His kind always does."

"Yeah," the first deputy said. "And we can charge him with a hundred or more murders. There's two more of them inside."

"If it were not for all these Klansmen's families, we wouldn't have a thing to go on, but after the other night, they all want him in jail."

"And I just wanted to talk to him..." said the Pinkerton man sarcastically.

It was two days after the mass funeral of his parents and friends that Jason began to think clearly. He prayed constantly for forgiveness for what he had said to his God that night on the battery. If anyone knew what pain and suffering were all about, it was his Lord and Savior, Jesus Christ. How could he be so numbed with pain and stupid to have said, or even thought, what he did?

And then, there were Meta's words to him that he had not really heard when she said them.

"Fitzsimmons Manigault was your father. Forgive me. Forgive me..."

"I do not condemn you, Mama," he whispered. "And I know in my heart God has forgiven you. Certainly I..."

Jason did not yet know how to react to the revelation Meta had made. First, that he was a bastard and secondly, his father was a white man.

"How could she be sure," he wondered. "Why didn't the elder Fitzsimmons even look at him somewhat differently than the other blacks? What had been done for him was done by Sophia, not Fitzsimmons. Of course, he had approved. Did Sophia know? Oh my God! Did Fitz know? Fitz had called him "brother" many times over the years. Was he being literal after all?

It was too much to ponder for too long at a time. "Perhaps," he thought, "it will come to me in parts...all of these answers. Perhaps even the right questions will come, too.

Fitz arrived two days later. As soon as had heard about the attacks, he terminated his business and headed for home.

"Jason!" He put his arms around the Bishop's frail body. "Jason, I am so sorry."

"Thank you, Fitz," he said simply. "I'm just glad you were in Norfolk."

"Well, I'm glad Mary and Catherine were. Is there something I can do, brother?"

"No, Fitz. Your being here is enough."

"I'm sorry I missed the funerals."

"It couldn't be helped. Reverend Franklin did an excellent job."

"I'm sure. Jason, you don't look well at all. Perhaps a few days, or weeks, away from here..."

"No, No, Fitz. There is so much to be done. I think, right now, work is what I need most."

"Very well. Work is what we'll do. I'll have the architect her tomorrow. Our next hospital will be the finest in the South. I promise you. We'll build it as a memorial to Abraham and Meta."

"Let's build it as a memorial, yes, but let's dedicate it to those who came so close, but missed being truly free."
"All of the Negroes murdered by the Klan?"
"No, all of the Negroes. Period."

CHAPTER 37

The months rolled past and major changes began to transform the lives of Jason and Fitz. Jason now spent most of his time traveling throughout the South making his diocese a close knit, caring, and purposeful organization. By the time Mary gave birth to Fitz's first child, a girl, Jason had fifteen hundred churches under his leadership. His time at the Church of the Three Crosses became almost nil. However, he had no problems with that. He had learned the art of leadership. The art of allowing his assistants to do the work while he made decisions and supervised. Fitz's private car had practically become his home. Were it not for its luxury and comport, the pace could have killed Jason. He had developed a nagging, dry cough, which periodically, would rack his body. He continued to lose weight.

Fitz was extremely concerned about his friend and did everything he could to help. The best doctors, the private train car, the best accommodations to be had. Of course, Fitz was busy too, his empire ever growing and expanding. He now owned huge holdings in textiles and agriculture as well as railroads and shipping. Had it not been for this gift of choosing the right people and letting them do their jobs he, too, would have been broken by his workload.

Fitz was probably the wealthiest and most respected businessman in the world. Jason, without a doubt, was the most beloved living black minister in the world. Fitz knew how to tower above his competitors, yet stay on a par with his people. Jason appeared to be the most humble of men, often ignored by those who did not know him. His simple dress and undemanding ways made him appear just one of the crowd. Yet, when he spoke, whether to a group or an individual, his charisma showed like the star of Bethlehem and attracted all to him with a compelling magnetism.

Half of the nation must have gasped in shock when Fitz and Mary asked Jason to christen their daughter at the Church of the Three Crosses.

The whites asked, "Did you hear that rich bastard is lettin' a nigger baptize his youngun in a nigger church?"

The blacks simply observed in awe that such a thing could, especially would, be done.

When Jason took the baby from Mary at the alter, he added to the ceremony. Holding the lily-white child in his boney, black hands he turned to the congregation.

"I ask but one thing of the Church of the Three Crosses and the Diocese of the Church of the Southern Cross. If you love me, if you love your church, if you love our God, you will swear you protection to this child. Jennifer Mary Fitzsimmons. Let her be the first of a new generation. Let her not be white or black. Let her only be a child of God. A child whom he loves and whom we love. May 'black' babies and 'white' babies never be born again, only children. May none of us ever destroy again. Only protect. I baptize thee, Jennifer, in the name of the Father, the Son and the Holy Ghost. And with the hope that thou are the first born of the true brotherhood of man. Amen."

The tears stained his cheeks as he handed her back to Mary.

"Mary, Fitz," he whispered. "She is a beautiful child. I love you both and I love her for herself as well as for being yours."

"Thank you, Jason. I mean, your Grace," Mary said through her tears.

"Thank you, brother," whispered Fitz.

After the service, there was a meal for the entire congregation. It may have been the first time in the history of the South that hundreds of blacks and whites sat down to a meal together. City, state, and federal officials, many of the South's leading businessmen and the most humble of black field hands sat together and held hands while Reverend Franklin said grace over the feast Fitz had provided.

Fitz, Jason, Mary and several others sat together at the head table. Fitz whispered in Jason's ear.

"Perhaps it's a beginning, Jason. Nobody has jumped up and left."

"I hope you're right, Fitz," Jason whispered back. "Maybe they won't hurry home to take a bath and wash their mouths out either."

They both laughed.

Yes, it was a first. But in spite of Fitz and Jason's hopes, the meal was strained too, and, for the most part, silent.

※※※

At that moment, in a back street shack in Mobile, Bobby T. was waking from a drunken stupor. Inside him the hate for Fitz continued to grow. In his mind, the Manigault name had become responsible for every misfortune he had ever suffered. From his window, he could see Manigault ships loading and unloading in the harbor.

"That niggah lovin' son of a bitch is everywhere!" he spat.

The woman with him cowered in the bed. In the short time they had been together, she had come to know him well. For reasons that she could not understand, he was subject to violent rages and often would vent his wrath on her with a brutal beating. But she stayed with him anyway. The house, as bad as it was, was warm and dry. He fed her, and he let her drink all the liquor she wanted. She accepted him and paid by taking his beatings and giving him sex whenever and however he demanded.

He tore the covers from the bed, leaving her exposed, naked, on the mattress. Jerking off his belt, he flogged her legs and back with the wide strip of leather, cursing, screaming, calling her filthy names and accusing her of every sinful act he could think of. Finally he stopped. As she lay there whimpering, afraid to move a muscle, lest he start again. She felt the warm wetness of his urine down her back stinging the lacerations. But there was still more abuse to come for the beating had aroused him. Pulling off his pants and mounting her from behind, he thrusted wildly and subjected her to yet another barrage of curses. She had not been ready and the pain was excruciating, but she dared not cry out or complain.

"You don like it?" He slapped the back of her head. So, she made sounds of ecstasy until he spent himself and collapsed back into his stupor on the bed beside her. Untangling herself, she got up and did what she could to stop the bleeding. She picked up a bottle and drank herself senseless in a matter of minutes to subdue the pain.

Once he had safely escaped the Carolinas, Bobby T., for months, had thought of nothing but how to get Fitz. He wanted Fitz to suffer. God, how he wanted to hurt him. To kill him slowly from the inside out.

"That bitch he's married to. Iffen I could git my hands on her." He relished the fantasy of raping her and cutting her throat while Fitz looked on hopelessly, tied to a chair. "Then I'd kill him slow," he thought. "Put out his eyes first, then maybe cut out his tongue. Maybe then I'd turn him loose and kill him after he got well. Maybe..."

Then the news came. He was in a waterfront saloon when he heard there was now an heir to the great Manigault empire. A girl. He almost drooled. His fantasies took a new twist. He wanted to see Fitz's eyes when he handed him his daughter on the tines of a pitchfork. He began planning in earnest. He would return to Charleston, hire a couple of good men, and kidnap the child. That should be easy pickins'. Then he would get Fitz to come get her... alone. He laughed out loud when he decided to take a Manigault ship to Charleston.

"You might as well git me there, nigga lover."

As usual, there was much Bobby T. did not think about in his plans. First and foremost, as always, Fitz was no fool.

It was to be two years before Bobby T. put his plans into action.

CHAPTER 38

"Anita, this is Mr. Manigault," said the Pinkerton man.

She was a Negro woman, tall and lithe with a pleasant smile.

"How do you do, Anita. It was good of you to come."

"It was my pleasure, Mr. Manigault."

"I'm sure the agency has briefed you well. After all, you were hand-picked by them, then by me.

"Yes, I am very much aware of what you require."

"Is it true what they tell me?" Fitz asked.

"I don't know exactly what they've told you, Mr. Manigault, but I am an excellent nurse. I am educated. I am well prepared to protect your daughter. Until this assignment, I was personal bodyguard to Princess Enid de Levier in Jamaica. There were four attempts on her life while she was in my charge. They all failed."

"And there are seven dead would-be assassins," the Pinkerton man interjected.

"My daughter may not be a real princess, but she is to me. It's not her fault that I am a very wealthy man and she is subject to being harmed by every demented mind that may want to blackmail me."

"I understand. Let me just say this. When she is in my charge, I will not hesitate to die for her."

"You have said enough. You're hired."

"How old is your daughter, sir?"

"She's almost two now, a lot to handle."

"No problem, Mr. Manigault. I like the spirited twos."

When she stood to shake Fitz's hand, he realized she was over six feet tall. She moved with the grace of a cat as she left the room and went with the Pinkerton man to assume her duties with Mary and Jennifer.

"I would estimate she's every thing they say she is," he mused, feeling better about Jennifer's safety.

But she alone was not enough to please Fitz. If he had a strength, it was layering his safety precautions. In addition to Anita, he would have two men close by any time Jennifer left the house. He would take no chances with his daughter. After all, guards had saved the Church of the Three Crosses. But didn't the gatlin gun really swing it? It was not foolish to have back up to keep an edge. In this case, Anita would be the edge he wanted. Anyone would be able to pick out the two burly bodyguards, but few would suspect that the nurse was even more lethal than the men.

It did not take long for Anita to ingratiate herself. Educated, witty, and genteel, she was adored by Jennifer. Mary found her fascinating. Even the salty Catherine was captivated. Anita could play dolls with Jennifer, introduce a new dish in the kitchen, help Mary with redecorating a part of the mansion, or discuss the classics with Catherine. All this and much more, with equal ease and expertise.

In matters of Jennifer's security, she was even more expert. She would not allow their outings to become routine, neither in where they went or when they went. She insisted no patterns be established. That included the dress and demeanor of the two bodyguards. She directed that they not dress like bodyguards, but occasionally like workmen who were on their way to a job. At times they would appear to be old men out for a stroll in the sun, but never as two threatening figures watching over Jennifer. If there was a tendency for the security measures to grow slack on the part of the household, it never affected Anita. There had been no problems. But she knew problems would come. Even though Anita knew nothing of Bobby T. Jordan, she could sense that there was a threat afoot. It was like a bad odor to her. The day Bobby T. landed in Charleston, her instincts told her to tighten the reins on her charge. She could sense the danger.

It was a gnawing feeling that began as fear deep in her subconscious and ate its way to her consciousness as a feeling of dread. Each time it did this her mind would react with an increased awareness of the surroundings and her mouth would form a snarl as the fear changed to dread and precipitated in anger and resolution. Had Bobby T. known Anita, he would probably have taken the next ship out for Europe.

But he did not know Anita. He only knew hate. It was a hate that he had fabricated and nurtured until it had taken control of his life. Now it drove him. His sick mind grew more evil each day as his hate for the Manigaults ate his sanity away and directed his every fiber toward revenge. Even though he could have cared less for his brother when Big Mambo killed him, he now thought of him as a great martyr, sacrificed at the alter of Manigault greed.

CHAPTER 39

Jason's progressive physical deterioration was becoming of increasing concern to all those near to him. Reverend Franklin, in particular, was one who could see the Bishop was expending more energy than he could ever hope to restore. He appeared at Fitz's office on a cool fall Charleston morning.

"I'm concerned, too, Reverend," Fitz said as he stood at the window watching the perpetual comings and goings of Manigault freighters.

"The truth is, Mr. Manigault, without his dynamic leadership the Diocese may die. All of his work will have been in vain."

"That's too much of a load for one man to carry."

"It is. Perhaps you could talk him into taking a rest, perhaps even a leave of absence. His presence and influence would still be felt."

"I could try. But Jason is hardheaded. God's work comes first with him. He does not see himself as important."

"Maybe the Diocese could make him a gift. Perhaps a voyage so he could rest."

In Fitz's mind, there flashed a scene from long, long ago. He and Jason were in their hideout by the river.

"Fitz, I love this spot. Someday I'm gonna build me a cabin right her and sit on the porch and watch the river for forever."

"That's not likely, Jason."

"Why not?"

"We're practically in the shadow of Manigault House. Papa wouldn't let you build a cabin here."

"The Lord works in strange and mysterious ways, Fitz." Jason smiled with a far away look in his dancing black eyes.

"Mr. Manigault? Do you agree?"

Fitz returned from his daydreaming.

"Reverend, I know exactly what we need to do. The church will give him a cabin, a vacation home so to speak. We'll build it on the river's edge in front of Manigault House."

"That will help?"

"Believe me, if we want him to take some time off, this will do it."

"I'll have to call a meeting of the deacons. Money is short, but I'm sure..."

"My secretary will give you a draft. Take it to Archibald Bradley. I'll stand for all expenses."

"That's not necessary. We can find the money."

"Ah, Reverend, but you have already found the money. It is time we cannot find. Tell Archibald he has two weeks. I don't care what it costs. I want you to present the cabin to him on Sunday, the 19th.

"Very well, Mr. Manigault. I'll see to it. And I want you to know that I, and my church and the Diocese, thank you from the bottom of our hearts."

"This settles only half of the problem. Getting him there, and keeping him there for a while, is the real challenge."

That afternoon, Jason was writing in his study. He dropped his pen and leaned back. Even though the afternoon was pleasantly cool, he pulled the blanket more tightly about himself and lay his head back against the chair.

"The pain will pass in a moment," he thought. "It always does." But it was coming more often and more severely and lasting longer.

Two blocks away Anita was strolling with Jennifer along the Battery. Anita barely noticed the guards, only glancing up to make sure they were in place. It was the shabbily dressed vagrant walking toward her who had her full attention. When he passed, he smelled of body odor and cheap whiskey. He did not look up. Even though Anita did not look back, she sensed it when he stopped, turned and watched her. She could feel his eyes on the back of her neck. She firmed her grip on the derringer in her muff. But the man turned and continued on his way. An hour later, she berated the two bodyguards for not being closer when the stranger passed Jennifer.

"If you see him on this street again, I want him picked up and checked out. Do you understand?"

They shook their heads 'yes'.

Bobby T. walked back to his room in an old abandoned building off Meeting Street. He went straight to his bottle of cheap whiskey. He sat at his littered table, cursing a rat that ran past, and took a long drink from the bottle. He now knew he could not do it alone. Practically always drinking, he was still sufficiently aware that he recognized that the "gardeners" were bodyguards. The tall, skinny nigger nurse had also received his evaluation. He decided he could break her in half with one smashing right to her ugly face. If not, he would blow her guts out and grab the child. Then Fitz would have to come to him. He drooled at the thought. He would kill them both. Then he would get the fancy Manigault wife and kill her too. But right now he needed help. Maybe there were two old Klansmen still around that he could use. He decided to check along the waterfront bars. He would find what he needed. But he had forgotten there were many of his old cohorts who wanted him dead.

His first stop was an old favorite bar on the waterfront. The place was as rundown as it had ever been. The same rough looking old man was still behind the bar. He looked around the room and recognized several of the customers. They all looked up, studied him for a moment, and went back to heir conversations. He walked to the bar and roughly ordered a whiskey. Then he looked into the mirror behind the bar. It had been a long time since he had looked in a mirror. He did not recognize what he saw. He was no longer the menacing, dangerous looking man he had once been. He looked old, and stooped. His beard, weeks without a trim, was a tangled mess. His hair hung loosely, greasily, around his ears. The alcohol had taken its toll. His eyes, once prominent and frightening, now were sunk deeply into hollow sockets. No wonder nobody knows me, he thought. He finished his drink and returned to his room. If he was to accomplish his mission, he needed to clean himself up and dry the alcohol out of his system. The look into the mirror left no doubt of that.

After a week, the nausea and the trembling subsided. He even began eating on a regular basis. Another several days passed and he visited a bathhouse, a barber, and a clothing store. In spite of his long bout with alcohol, he still had a respectable sum of money that he had stolen from the Klan.

Now he returned to the bar, bright eyed, neatly trimmed, dressed n black and heavily armed. When he walked through the door, the men looked up. But this time they did not look away. Silence filled the room. Bobby T. looked from one to another of them, his eyes burning into them. Without exception, they could not stare back, but diverted their eyes to the floor.

"Is there a man left among you?" he spat.

No one responded.

"McKay! I'm talkin' to you, boy."

"I don't want no trouble with you, Jordan."

"I didn't come for trouble. I need two good men."

"For what?"

"Some easy money."

"Legal?" another man asked.

"Since when do any of ya'll care about legal? I need two men with guts. If you gotta ask legal, you're gutless."

For a moment the man was visibly angered. Then Bobby pulled his coat back, exposing his pistol belt.

"Well?"

No one spoke. Bobby wheeled and left the bar, cursing under his breath. He was barely a block away when someone called him from an alley. It was an old cohort named Jamie Graham. Bobby remembered him. He was ignorant, inept, gutless, but he fancied hiself as being smart and brave. He looked as unkempt as Bobby T. had a few days earlier.

"What do you want, Jamie?"

"The job."

Bobby hesitated. "Nah, this 'un ain't fer you."

"What do you mean? I'm the best man you ever had."

"You son of a bitch. You didn't even show up for the church raid."

"I wuz sick. You know I wuz sick. I wuz so sick that night I couldn't set a horse."

"You wuz so scared you couldn't set a horse."

"Iffen I'da been there we'd o' won."

"I ain't got time for you. I need two real men."

"You ain't gonna find nobody else. Mos' of 'em want to put a bullet in you anyhow."

"They ain't got the guts t try."

"Please, Bobby T. I need the money."

"Listen her, boy, you don't even know what we goin' to do or what I'm willin' to pay."

"It don't matter. I can handle anything. An' I know you'll pay me fair."

Bobby T. hesitated for a long minute. Then he reached in his pocket and took out a gold coin.

"Here, go git yo' self cleaned up and git some decent clothes. For this job you gotta look like a gentleman."

"Thank you, Bobby. I will... I will..."

"Meet me here tomorrow at one o'clock."

"I'll be here. I swear I will."

"Jamie, you drink that up and I'll find you and split our gullet. You understand?"

"Don't worry. One o'clock. I'll be here lookin' like one of them fellers what live on the Battery."

"Exactly."

Jamie was true to his work. When Bobby rounded the corner the next afternoon at one, he barely recognized him. He was clean, dressed and sober.

"Awright, Jamie. We gonna take a stroll."

They started down Meeting Street toward the Battery.

"What's the job?"

"Jest be patient and walk, boy."

They turned the street onto the Battery just as Anita and Jennifer were leaving the house.

"See that niggah and youngun? Damn it; don't look at them so hard. They'll see you lookin'."

"I see 'em, Bobby. I see 'em."

"That there youngun-I want her."

"Fer what?"

Bobby gave him a withering glare. "Never you mind how come. Jest listen. See that man leaning on the rail down yonder? He's a bodyguard. There's another on walkin' up the street behind us."

Jamie turned to look behind him.

"Damn it don't turn around, you fool! We're strollin', we ain't lookin'."

"I'm sorry, Bobby."

The niggah, she takes the youngun out most good days. I been watchin' from the bushes for weeks. I even walked down the street pass 'em once. We gotta take out the bodyguards and the niggah and snatch the youngun. That's the job."

The air went out of Jamie.

"Well?"

"I don't know."

"You son of a bitch, you're in or you're a dead man. I didn't tell you this for you to turn me in for no reward."

"How...how much?"

"A hundred dollars. Now shut up. They're comin'."

They both nodded to Anita and Jennifer when they passed. Anita's defenses were bristling, but she didn't know why. It would have been impossible for her to recognize Bobby T. as the same man who half staggered past her just weeks before. Today he was not in rags, nor in black. He looked like a banker from downtown rather than a renegade. But there was a threat in the air and Anita could feel it.

Back in the smelly, disorderly room, the two men sat down at the table.

"I want a carriage and two good strong horses. And we gonna need two saddle horses. We'll leave the carriage here. We take the saddle horses to the Battery and dismount and wait. When we see the guards, I get on my horse and go to the far one; you walk to the close one. When you git to him, you put a knife in his belly. I'll shoot the other one and the niggah and scoop up the youngun. You git on your horse and we high tail it back her and take the carriage an' git out of town."

"It's gonna be risky, Bobby."

"Risky, hell! We take the goons by surprise and they ain't nobody left but the skinny niggah mammy. You scared of a skinny niggah mammy?"

"No. Nothin' scares me."

CHAPTER 40

Fitz was called away from Charleston on the 17th to an emergency in Savannah. Much to his regret, he would miss the church's presentation of the cabin to Jason.

"No need to worry about it," he told Reverend Franklin. "It's your show anyway and I know you and the deacons will do it right."

There was a chill in the air when the line of carriages left the Church of the Three Crosses on the morning of the nineteenth. Jason was wrapped snuggly in a shawl over his topcoat in the back seat of the lead carriage. He was told they were to open a new church near the Manigault. It was always his policy to bless a new sanctuary. Today, he was particularly anxious to go. He might get a glimpse of the Manigault.

It was still a four-hour trip. Jason, his strength very low, was extremely tired when the carriage turned into the Manigault. In spite of his weariness, he sat up in his seat.

"You said near the Manigault, Matthew. Did you mean on the Manigault?"

Reverend Franklin grinned like a child. "Yes, this temple is on the Manigault, your Grace."

When they rounded the house, there were people, mules, and wagons everywhere. They all began to applaud and greet the Bishop's entourage.

When the carriage stopped, Jason stood and waved to the crowd. Then he saw Mrs. Manly standing on the porch of a beautiful, not so small, cabin. Feelings and thoughts rushed over him. He didn't remember it being there. Especially there, right squarely over his and Fitz's favorite hideout on the water's edge.

The crowd grew silent. You could hear the wind in the trees."

"Your Grace," Reverend Franklin said, "We are your people. You have given us of yourself without hesitation, without condition, without hope of return all of your adult life. Today, we, your people in some small, insignificant measure, give something back to you. This is our gift to you. A summer home. A retreat. A place where you can rest and commune with God."

Then Reverend Franklin smiled and said in a low voice to Jason. "Now you have three possessions, Jason. A Bible, a knife, and a cabin."

Jason stood in the carriage. He looked from face to face among the hundreds of well-wishers around him. Tears flowed, but he was unashamed.

"My beloved people, you make it impossible to refuse. This is the place I was born. And, thanks to you, it will be the place I die. Two wonderful life times, for me, will have begun here. Thank you, and God bless each of you." Then he sat, too weak to continue standing.

Reverend Franklin and Mrs. Manly helped Jason down from the carriage and into the cabin as the celebration began. There were games for the children, the older folks rested in the sun and talked, and the young people strolled hand-in-hand along the water's edge. A feast of fried chicken and pork ribs with all the trimmings was set out for everyone.

Inside the roomy, comfortably furnished cabin it was quiet as Mrs. Manly served tea to Jason and the Deacons.

"Alright, Matthew, where did all the money come from?" Jason asked.

"Now, your Grace, that's not an appropriate question."

"Matthew?"

"Your Grace, where does the money always come from?"

Jason smiled as more tears glistened in his eyes.

"Word says Manigault is out of town," Bobby T. said absentmindedly.

"What?"

"Nothin', Jamie. These the best horses you could find?"

"They is. And the carriage is new."

"Yeah. The carriage is OK. Stow this blanket. We'll tie the youngun in it."

"When we goin' to do it?"

"This afternoon."

"Already?"

"Better sooner than later. I don't want you to chicken out and run."

"I ain't gonna chicken out! You know me, Bobby T."

"Yeah. I know you, Jamie. I wish the hell we had one more man, but the two of us can manage if you hold up your end."

"You can count on me. Uh...you want to pay me now?"

"You'll get paid when the job is done."

"Fine. That's fine."

At two o'clock, they were in place at the end of the Battery. Their horses were tied and they sat on a bench talking like two ordinary businessmen.

No one came out of the house. No bodyguard appeared.

Three o'clock. Still no one.

Three thirty.

"They ain't comin' and we been here too long. Let's go."

They mounted and returned to Meeting Street. They had barely turned the corner when Anita and Jennifer emerged for their outing. Bobby T. and Jamie had not noticed the two fishermen who were now climbing onto the shore.

"You spending the night, Jamie?" Bobby T. asked when they reached the room.

"What happened, Bobby?"

"Who knows. Maybe the brat got sick. We'll do it again tomorrow."

"OK. Can't we git some of these damn rats out o' here?"

The next afternoon it was raining.

"Ain't no good to go. Jest get wet," Bobby said looking through the open door. "They ain't comin' out in this."

The next day was sunny. The renegades checked their weapons and headed for the Battery. When they turned the corner, Anita and Jennifer were heading back to the house. There was no time to stop.

"Take the first one," Bobby T. said to Jamie as he spurred his horse.

Jamie spurred his animal, too. But there would be no knifing. The near guard, hearing the clatter of Bobby's horse's hooves turned to see him charging past with his pistol held high. Instinctively, he pulled his weapon and dropped to his knee, taking careful aim at Bobby T. But before he could fire, a 44-caliber pistol ball entered his back and emerged through his ribcage with a burst of blood, bone, and guts. The impact knocked the guard to his face. For a moment, he tried to get up, and then flopped lifelessly.

The far guard, hearing the commotion, whirled and began firing at the charging Bobby T. A Bullet struck the horse in the neck. His eyes glared, his nostrils flared, but he continued to respond to the spurs. Bobby emptied his gun at the second guard. The last two rounds were true. The guard appeared surprised, then collapsed with a puzzled stare still on his face.

Anita, having decided that getting the child to safety was wiser than defending against the attackers, swept up Jennifer and was running towards the house. By the time, Jamie's horse passed Bobby T. and was closing in on them. Realizing she couldn't make it to the house, Anita stopped and turned. She pushed Jennifer to the side and pulled her derringer from its concealed place. Jamie was practically on top of her when one well-placed shot tore through his skull and knocked him out of the saddle. The maddened animal knocked Anita off her feet and in its confusion, trampled her, reared, and fell back upon her.

Jennifer, not understanding, stood and watched. Bobby reached down and jerked her across the saddle and turned up Travis Street before the people began emerging from their homes.

In less than a minute, four people were dead.

Within an hour, the house was swarming with Pinkerton men. Fitz, informed by telegraph, was in a fast packet from Savannah. Bobby T., with Jennifer, had disappeared. Jamie was identified before the sun set. But it was not helpful. He was only one of the dozens of riff-raff that populated the Charleston dock area.

The following morning a sinister looking letter arrived by post for Fitz. He arrived home in the afternoon. After consoling Mary and listening to the total frustration of the police and the Pinkertons, he opened the letter.

Manigault,

If you want yo chile, you come to Johnson's mill on the Pee Dee at 5 o'clock on Friday. Come alone. Bring $10,000 gold. I'll kill her if you don't.

"He's cut it close. That's tomorrow afternoon," Fitz said

"That will be rushing our planning," the Pinkerton man said.

"There will be no planning, Fredericks," Fritz said. "Ten thousand dollars is nothing."

"Are you sure it's the money he wants? I think it's you."

"Why?" Fitz asked.

"Bobby T. is in town. He was seen in the Honey Bear bar last week."

"If this is Bobby T., it's high time we met again," Fitz responded. Then he turned to his chief executive officer of Manigault Shipping.

"Grimes, get me ten thousand in gold."

"Yes, sir. Right away."

CHAPTER 41

Fitz left for Johnson's mill before daylight. It was a long ride and he dared not be late.

When he arrived, he was in somewhat of a dilemma. He didn't want to sneak up on the man, yet he thought to just ride up would be an invitation to being shot. He had been working on a plan throughout the entire morning. About a hundred yards from the mill he dismounted. He put the saddlebags of money at the foot of a giant oak, and then proceeded on foot. He was careful to stay behind his horse just enough to make a poor target.

Arriving at the abandoned mill he stopped.

"Jordan!"

No answer.

"Jordan! It's Fitz Manigault. I'm alone. I have your money. Get my daughter out here!"

Bobby T. appeared in the doorway. Jennifer was with him. He held a handful of her hair tightly in one hand and in the other he held a pistol.

"You betta be alone, boy!" Or this is one dead brat."

"I'm alone."

"How'd you know hit were me?"

"I knew."

"Then git you ass up here and bring the money."

Fitz dropped his reins and walked to the door of the mill.

"Where's the money? I don't see none."

"It's down the road a bit. You don't thing I would be that stupid to bring it with me do you?"

Bobby T.'s eyes narrowed. "I think you really want this youngun dead."

"And I think you want the money and both of us dead."

"Git the money! Now!"

"Give me the child."

"You ain't in no position to be givin' orders here, boy. Open your coat."

Fitz did as he said and opened his coat. Jordan could see that he was not armed.

"I'll give you the brat when you give me the money"

"You've got the gun so give her to me now and I'll lead you to the money."

Bobby T. hesitated and scanned the forest around them.

"Awright. But one funny move and I'll shoot both of you. And I'll shoot her first."

Bobby T. pushed Jennifer towards Fitz, but kept his gun on her. Fitz picked her up and slowly walked back down the small wagon road as Bobby T. followed warily about ten feet back. When he reached the tree, he put Jennifer down beside it.

"Sit here, Honey," Fitz said as he motioned for her to sit behind the tree trunk.

"The money's over there, Jordan."

"Git it!" Bobby T. spat.

Fitz walked over to the tree and reached down for the saddlebags. With his left hand he held the saddlebags high so Bobby T. could see them. With his right hand, he came up with the Colt pistol that he had hidden there and put a bullet in Bobby T.'s right shoulder, sending him spinning backwards and knocking his weapon out of his hand. Bobby T. pawed at his belt for his other pistol. A second bullet tore out his right lung and his arm went limp. He must have passed out, for the next thing he saw was Fitz standing over him.

"Where's my mother, Jordan?"

In spite of the pain and the blood pouring from his mouth, Bobby T. laughed.

"Buried in Bailey's Grove. Ha! Only a mile for the Manigault. Do you want to know what I done to her before I kilt her, boy?"

The explosion was deafening when the Colt blew out the back of Jordan's head.

Fitz looked down at the faceless, emaciated body. A strange feeling of disappointment and revulsion passed over him. He was disappointed that there was no feeling of elation or victory from finally dealing with this vermin. His feeling of revulsion was toward himself for having been required to stoop so low, for having to respond to the most basic animalistic part of himself to simply protect those he loved from the very thing he had done. He wondered, "Who are the real evil ones in this world? If I'm capable of this, am I not one of them?"

CHAPTER 42

Fitz wrapped himself in his work. He needed to escape this person- himself-that he really did not know at all. Often he wondered if Bobby T. hadn't been the real victor after all.

⁂

It was a cold, dreary afternoon when Fitz heard a commotion in his outer office. When he opened the door he saw a worried looking Reverend Franklin.

"Mr. Manigault. Please, you must come. The Bishop is gravely ill. He's at the cabin."

"Has the doctor been called?"

"He's been with him for hours. He sent me for you."

"You go ahead, Matthew. I'll be right behind you."

Fitz rode hard from Charleston towards Jason's cabin. He stopped his horse when he reached the oak-lined lane that lead into the Manigault. The moon was now high in the star-filled sky. He had not been here since he left so many years ago for England. His feelings were mixed. His heart pounded with anticipation, yet there was a saddening dread that overcame him, a terrible foreboding. So many happy memories were here, and so much hurt over the terrible loss of his parents, the passing of a carefree childhood...

He started his mount at a slow walk up through the ancient stately oaks that guarded the place where his heart would always live. Inside the trees, the lane was dark, but the moon cast a light through the openings in the branches like millions of sparkling diamonds spilling down to be crushed beneath the horse's hooves. He listened intently to the silence. Was it the wind, or did he truly hear the sound of children's voices playing and laughing.

"We done blood pacted 'bout everything..." he heard Jason say.

"Fitz, the tutor is here. You have to come in now..." he could hear his mother call.

"Yes, Mama. I'm coming."

"You boys be careful with that raft...you hear?"

"Yes, Papa, we will."

He heard the sounds of the darkies singing. How wonderful they were.

It was only when he reached the end of the lane and Manigault House stood before him, huge, stark and looming, that he realized it was only the wind and that he had only been listening to his heart.

He stopped. Manigault House looked down at him. How magnificent she was! How desperately cold and lonely she looked. She was dead inside now. No light shone through her windows, no warmth exuded from her once proud doors with their heavy brass furnishings. Nevertheless, she was still impressive. And she still harbored the echoes of a life style that would never again grace the earth. He looked to his mother's beloved rose garden, now a tangle of weeds and briars. The statuary was gone, or broken, or over grown with vines.

There was so much beauty here, he thought. It should be brought back. In an instant, he resolved to rebuild her. No, not rebuild. He would restore her to the splendor she had known. If his mother's ghost was here, and his father's too, then they shall walk her halls as she should be, not as a wrecked hulk.

"Massa Fitz? Dat be you? Praise the Lord! Massa Fitz, dat be you!"

In an instant he returned from a world a million miles away, a million years past.

"Who's that?"

"It be Mattie, Massa Fitz."

"Mattie? My God, I thought you were dead!"

"Nawsuh. I been here all along. I ain't neber lef'."

"Well, we'll take you back to the church. They'll take good care of you."

"Dey say he dyin', Massa. Dey say Jason's dyin'."

"Let's hope not, Mattie. Perhaps the doctors will help this time."

"I hep bring him into this worl'. Lord, dat wuz some night. Yo' daddy was beside hisself, two sons comin' into dis world together. Eber now and den, he'd come from de house to de quarters and check on numba two."

"Mattie, what are you talking about?"

"You ain't know?"

"Know what?"

"Dat you and Jason be haf brothers."

"No, I didn't know."

"Lord, maybe I shouldn't of said nothing. I..."

"Does Jason know?"

"I ain't rightly know, but I reckon he do."

"I'd better go to Jason. Now you stay close. You're going back to Charleston with us."

"Yas suh."

Fitz dismounted and led his horse around the back of the house. The back yard was ablaze with torches. Dozens of people sat quietly watching the cabin door. Soft sobs could be heard. Other than the quiet mourning of those present, the torches burned in silence.

Fitz entered the cabin. Inside the grief was the same. The leaders of the Diocese of the Southern Cross sat in mute silence, praying, or just staring into emptiness.

"Fitz," Mrs. Manly whispered. "He's in his bedroom. He wants you to come right in."

Fitz went in and sat by him. He looked at the emaciated man lying under the quilts. He could feel his heart breaking. On the bedside table was Jason's Bible and jack knife. Fitz picked up the tattered book. It was limp in his hand from a thousand reading and another thousand sermons. Quietly, he laid it back in its place.

Jason opened his eyes.

"Fitz!"

"Hello, little brother."

Jason smiled.

"What's this I hear you're not feeling well."

"Rumors, my friend. Just vicious rumors."

Fitz reached down and took Jason's frail hand in his.

"You'll get better. You're just tired. The doctors can't find anything wrong. A good rest and you'll be fine."

"I'm sorry, Fitz. It won't be that way. Not this time."

"Sure it will."

"I'm worried about the church."

"Don't. I pledge my support. I'll endow it for a hundred years n my will. You don't have to worry."

"Thank you, friend. If my guardian angel is going to look after it, it will be all right."

"No problem, little brother. Now we have to get you well."

"You have been the best friend that any man, black or white, has ever known, Fitz. Heaven must be full of people like you. I'll save your place there. I promise."

"I'm not sure I'll get there."

"Of course you will."

It was no time to bring up Bobby T. but it was on Fitz's mind.

"Jason, brother of mine, I love you."

"And I love you, my brother. Now, let us speak of other things."

"But you are my brother, Jason. Jason? Jason!"

His small hand had gone limp. There had been no struggle, no pain. His face reflected that he was at peace. Tears welled in Fitz's eyes and tumbled shamelessly down his cheeks. He reached down and picked his brother up and carried him from the room, through the front of the house and onto the porch. For a long moment, he stood on the porch with Jason cradled in his arms, his head nestled in the hollow of his shoulder. The blacks gathered around him. Not a word was spoken. Finally Fitz said in a crackling whisper: "Friends, my brother has gone to more important work. But he is not dead. He will live forever in the love he has spread among us.

Still, there was overwhelming silence. Then, as the torches flickered and danced over a hundred faces, an old woman began a soft hymn. One by one the voices joined her, creating a soft, harmonious stairway for the soul of Jason Appelligo–the first black Bishop–to ascend to the throne of his father, God almighty.

ABOUT THE AUTHOR

John Fleetwood Moody, to some John, to others "Fleet", was born in Lake City, South Carolina. That's about sixty miles west of Myrtle Beach, certainly not east. He graduated from The Citadel with a degree in English and holds a Masters in Counseling degree with many additional hours in Psychology. He is a Licensed Professional Counselor (LPC). He retired from the US Army as a lieutenant Colonel after twenty-two years of flying small aircraft and helicopters including two tours in Viet Nam. Since then, he has worked as a Marriage and Family Counselor and in the drug addictions field in South Carolina.

ABOUT GREATUNPUBLISHED.COM

greatunpublished.com is a website that exists to serve writers and readers, and remove some of the commercial barriers between them. When you purchase a greatunpublished.com title, whether you receive it in electronic form or in a paperback volume or as a signed copy of the author's manuscript, you can be assured that the author is receiving a majority of the post-production revenue. Writers who join greatunpublished.com support the site and its marketing efforts with a per-title fee, and a portion of the site's share of profits are channeled into literacy programs.

So by purchasing this title from greatunpublished.com, you are helping to revolutionize the publishing industry for the benefit of writers and readers.
And for this we thank you.